Harbourtown Murder

Author's Note

This was a challenge for me, four years on from my first NaNoWriMo where I wrote a complete book in 18 days. I wanted to do something special as part of a fundraiser for the MacMillan run The Grove Hotel in Bournemouth. National Novel Writing Month is traditionally in November each year but as they are a charitable organisation I couldn't do this challenge at the time they stipulated, therefore I didn't have the support of my fellow writers while tackling the 50,000 word novel challenge.

As I do not enjoy good health, I was very limited as to what sort of fundraiser I could do - thus when I thought of the new book idea of NaNoWriMo, I was excited. I am however more ill now than I was four years ago when I last attempted this - and I am amazed to say that I did equal the record!

Last year we discovered my father has cancer of the oesophagus and he has had such great care and treatment, we as a family are so grateful for everything that has been done for him. Recovery, of course, is lengthy and complex - we'd never heard of The Grove until last year and I just love the idea of the hotel, a place to retreat from the stress and strain of your illness.

We are of course very fortunate that we do not have to pay medical costs in this country, and there are many charitable causes that are all worthy. My thanks go to the Manager, Brenden, who does an excellent job of running the hotel and dealing with all queries, including lots from me!

I raised £260. I honestly do not mind how it was spent as I know it was useful to them. Sadly, it is now closed.

I haven't managed - until now - to write a proper murder mystery, so I hope nobody is disappointed by this offering! With this in mind, I have asked my writer friend, Stephen E J Tomporowski, to help me to ensure that the best story goes out to the world.

Our roles have been reversed, I first encouraged Steve to write his own books several years ago and I edit them - he has learned writing and editing, and designing and formatting skills while under my tutelage.

Harbourtown is set on the Cornish coast, around the Marazion/Penzance area. It is purely fictional as are the characters. I have consulted many websites to get the information required to make the book as correct as I can including WikiPedia, the RNLI website, Cornish Birding website and others.

Enjoy!
      Yvonne

PS - It is interesting to note that Venus was the name given to my father in his Royal Navy days, and as one legendary story goes, the Queen Mother knew him by it!

Epilogue

The catly shadow fell across the lit cobblestone quayside as Felix the lighthouse flooded the area with its beams. On and off all night, or only for as long as necessary. Vimto was the lighthouse cat of Harbourtown island, but his story started on Conning mainland.

The stray had been watching the shoreline for weeks. It not only provided rich pickings in regard to food morsels, drinking puddles and discarded food stuffs; but also entertainment. Every day something new washed up on the beach - bits of fish or crabs, seashells, seaweed, bits of netting and wires and ropes. Some things were better than others.

He also kept an eye on the locals - the humans all interacted, all smiling and waving and friendly, so he decided to try to get close to some. Maybe someone would adopt him; maybe they would just feed him; maybe they would stop and make a fuss for a few minutes. Whatever.

His siblings had been taken away by the animal man; he'd arrived out of the blue with a large net and an even larger pen, shoving them all inside by the scruffs of their necks and slamming the door shut. But he wasn't going to be caught like that! Hiding in the shadows, he listened to his family howling as the van drove off with them. He knew he'd be alone from now onwards, but it meant less competition for humans, food, shelter and adventure.

Strutting his stuff when the coast was clear, he went first to visit his usual haunts before finding the better territories of his former siblings.

Weeks of scouring the area had him discover all the great places - and kind people who wanted to make a fuss. Soon, he had established a routine, and come rain or shine, he always ensured he made a daily beach trawl.

He recognised the man of the weird cushioned craft. The man and this weird contraption were regular visitors to the mainland, to-ing and fro-ing several times a day; the cat's gaze followed the man travelling to the next island, watching as he disappeared from view.

Hours later, he returned again. He was a nice man: often stopping to say hello, stroking him sometimes; even once, pulling along a piece of string the cat had found so that they could play.

There were a few humans with boats who stopped to talk and fuss; the cat made sure that he purred and pressed himself against them. They seemed to appreciate the gestures and reciprocated the affection. Nobody shouted at him whenever he was exploring their boats.

He loved the smells - some fishy, some oily, some he couldn't recognise. The humans allowed him to sniff for however long he wanted before telling him that it was time to go. He always hopped out again onto the shingly sand without needing to be chased away. It became another part of the beach routine.

Curious, the cat went to the cushioned part of the man's boat and sniffed when nobody was around. It didn't smell like a normal boat, but it certainly could move - he'd seen it zip across the water at speed. He wondered what it was like on board, would it be the same as the other boats? With nobody watching, he hopped in to explore. It was comfortable and so, he found a place to settle down out of the way.

It wasn't long before the man returned and the thing

started up. Uncurling himself, he yawned and stretched before going to explore further. The sea was smooth meaning the journey wasn't too bumpy. Also looking over the side was easy.

The sea spray in his face was quite different - cold and salty, so not any good for drinking - but nonetheless pleasing. Head up, nose in the air, tail curled around his paws, the cat was enjoying the trip out in the weird boat.

The man shouted suddenly then. Alarmed, the cat jumped: opening his eyes, he saw the man in front of him, gesturing and waving.

"How did you get here?" Yves frowned.

"Meow." The cat replied.

"I can't turn back now. You'll have to stay for the ride." His serious face turned into a smile. "You'll be safe, just don't try to jump into the water okay?" Gently, he patted the top of his head and the cat gave him a smile. Yves could've sworn it was a smile...

And so, the cat travelled on the vessel regularly. Sometimes the man looked for him, sometimes he didn't. Where the man and his boat lived - on the largest of the islands off the mainland - the cat decided he too would live there. On the return journey to the mainland, the cat didn't appear as usual.

Worried when he hadn't seen the creature for a few days, Yves was relieved to see the cat on the island's beach, happily sniffing along as he'd seen him do at Conning. He waved when the cat looked up and could've sworn the cat smiled back at him again.

He didn't dare tell his partner about the animal. She would want to take over and have him sent back, or picked up by the shelter people, or worse. He decided - for now - to allow the cat to live on the island, but kept an eye on him.

There were no other cats or any predators around, so he was safe on Harbourtown island. Live and let live, the man told himself.

During the storm the following day, Yves wondered where the cat had taken refuge. As the beacon from the lighthouse flashed across the harbour, he saw an unusual shape in the light. He then recognised the catly shadow - the cat was safely in the lighthouse! Smiling to himself as he closed the door behind him, he knew he had been right to let the animal find his own way.

The next morning, he saw again the cat was on the beach. A family had spread themselves out on the sand and the cat was making friends. Stopping off to see them, the cat recognised him - running up to him, purring and rubbing himself around his legs.

"Is he your cat?" The children asked him.

Yves shook his head, bending down to rub the cat's head, "he lives in the lighthouse."

"Cool!" They exclaimed. "What's his name?"

Yves frowned. "I don't know."

"He must be a mixed breed." The parent spoke then.

"Mixed up, like Vimto!" The children spoke together, laughing.

The oldest child took a juice bottle out of their picnic basket when Yves frowned in confusion. "See? Vimto is made of mixed fruits." He pointed out the label.

"Like the cat. Look, even his eyes are mixed." The youngest said.

"Meow!" The cat declared loudly.

"That's a great name." Yves agreed. "What do you think, boy?" He asked the cat.

"Meow!" Came the agreement.

Fast Forward

Vimto was in the warm and dry, up in the lighthouse. As much as he wanted to go out on his afternoon stroll - it was becoming increasingly lucrative day by day as more people offered him treats - he was not going out in that. No animal would, not even the daftest human would.

Slipping and sliding on the treacherous cobblestoned quayside of the harbour as they desperately dashed for cover, the last of the humans disappeared from view. The beacon from the lighthouse started to flash, warning all who saw it.

Out of the corner of his eye, he saw two figures in waterproofs below. They were pushing each other; any noises were drowned out by the thunder overhead. Something glinted in the flash of lightning above them: in the next moment, one figure slumped to the ground and the other ran off. Another lightning flash and gust of wind displayed the face of the human fleeing the scene: it was one Vimto recognised well.

The storm blew over after an hour; Vimto remained on watch, keeping an eye on the prone figure: it was unmoving and undisturbed by anyone as the storm raged, keeping people inside for the duration.

Chapter 1

The Treduggan family decided if they were to open up the family house gardens on Harbourtown to visitors, then they really should capitalise on having the tourists disturb their peace.

Cornwall as a rule thrives on tourism, and Conning mainland with the eight islands clustered around it was no different. What could they do that would be both profitable and viable? Which location would work best, both for visitors and for the family?

This needed careful planning...

Renovations planned over the next year would turn the lower barn areas and adjoining ramshackle building into an Inn, and a café. This was situated in an ideal position - several hundred yards from the harbour and, perhaps more importantly, slightly over a mile from the family home perched on top of the mountainous rise in the midst of the island.

Gossip found the plans over ambitious - an Inn and a café?! Surely only one would be required. Nowadays most pubs offered hot drinks and cakes, therefore wasn't both an oversight? The short trip over to Harbourtown on the hovercraft from Conning meant that overnight stays weren't necessary, although the Inn would be built with two rooms for guests. Living quarters for the innkeeper's family and the café owner were to be built above each of the premises, it was learned. Those selected by the Treduggan family to run the premises would be expected to move to Harbourtown, despite the near vicinity to Conning. It was another point that sparked up gossip.

Decades ago, Harbourtown was built off the coast of Conning to allow ships to dock safely in order for their goods to be transferred to the mainland by local, smaller craft. With half of the beach at Conning given over to mudflats, and the rest of the area blocked off by the danger of the rocky shoreline, hovercraft was the best and fastest solution to provide the link between the two.

Harbourtown boasted a working harbour and also a still working lighthouse to warn incoming ships of the rocky coastline ahead. Any ship not knowledgeable of this part of the coast soon found out about the lurking dangers before it was too late. Harbourtown's Royal National Lifeboat Institution (RNLI) team worked tirelessly to prevent ships running aground at Conning. Signs on land and buoyancy aids in the water were more precautions, and to date it had been several years since a ship had been lost on the rocks.

The local lifeboat service used an inshore lifeboat and a hovercraft, both kept at Harbourtown in order to be ready to launch at a moment's notice. RNLI presence along the British coast is not an unusual sight, even if the town doesn't have a lifeboat station, it will undoubtedly have lifeguards on duty at particular times. A deep pride swells in the breast of everyone associated with the RNLI, no matter their job title. As well as going out on rescues, lifeboat crew members also commit to regular training in boat handling, radio communications, casualty care, navigation and radar. It always amazes the public to learn that most crew members are volunteers from local communities - a coxswain, a helm or commander, a mechanic and various other crew members make up a lifeboat team.

Ergo, Harbourtown came into existence and remained of extreme importance to this part of the Cornish coast.

Chapter 2

Walter Copper was the local policeman. Living on the mainland, he made frequent trips out to Harbourtown and neighbouring Roundhouse Island as part of his beat using his boat, Lady Sybil.

Whereas Harbourtown was industrial, Roundhouse was regarded as leisurely, thanks to the three cousins, Hope, Faith and Joy Anchorage, who ran an arty vacation haven there. Nobody knew why it was called Roundhouse as the island was 3 metres square.

Patrons of Roundhouse island created masterpieces of painting and photography: there was a gallery of previous visitor's work and a small shop also, as well as the accommodations on the island. Each accommodation was a quaint fisherman's cottage, restored with all mod cons, and boasting its own veranda. The artists could set up an easel on the deck to paint whenever inspiration struck if they so wished.

There were structured lessons for guests who wanted to paint - landscapes and scenic, portraits and figural work, and introductions to working with different mediums. Those interested in photography were taught the basics as well as the more complex techniques, and given one-to-one specialised training.

The main building on Roundhouse was cool and airy, but warm in worse weather - this was the combination lecture and restaurant area, with a quiet space separated for those seeking peace to study and experiment.

As plagued part of the mainland, one stretch of the beach was taken over by mudflats, but the largest beach area, situated right outside the main building, stretched around the island so that views of both the sunrise and sunset could be sought. All in all, it truly was an artists' paradise!

The local policeman wasn't the only one who visited each day in his boat, Yves the ferryman, if he could have that title as his ferry was a hovercraft, also was a regular visitor. He brought them provisions from the mainland, mostly art and food supplies, and also regularly presented the groups with talks on the local wildlife and of coastal safety, and the importance of the RNLI volunteer service.

It was his idea to start tours for birders - the other islands nearby were all uninhabited and had become overridden by wildlife. Seal Point was the largest of these islands, sporting - despite the name - few seals, when they weren't alongside the fishing boats inside Harbourtown sheltered harbour area. Yves suspected that in the past there had been a plethora of seals basking in the sunlight there: the name had perhaps been a logical one, once upon a time.

Mostly Seal Point was a home to birdlife, some on home territory, but also offering a temporary residency to more exotic species blown off course by strong winds during their migratory journeys. Recorded sightings over the years showed that this happened with frequency. That fact alone stood them in good stead!

The other islands were too small to be of much use to humans; no more than scraps of land amongst a collection of rocks jutting out above sea level. However, they proved to be perfect bird sanctuaries. Throughout local history nobody had bothered to name the small rocky islands, they were simply related to as islands 4, 5, 6, 7 and 8.

Harbourtown was the largest of the islands at approximately 9 miles circumference, followed in size by Roundhouse, and then Seal Point consisting of around one and a half miles.

It was not unusual to have unnamed, uninhabited islands around the Cornish coastline. Other than the famous Isles of Scilly there are several islands, or small inlets, such as St Michael's Mount, Looe Island, Godrevy Island, Eddystone Rocks and Town Island. Of note, Lundy and Drake's Island were commonly referred to as Cornish but are actually Devon islands.

All of this would fit into the general talk about their coastal home, Yves knew. His partner Caitlin was a green-fingered goddess, the Treduggan family gardener on Harbourtown. Her plant knowledge could play a part in nature talks. She too loved following the progress of the migrating birds as they wheeled and swooped in the air above their heads - this made her the ideal candidate for hosting the birders tours.

Hmm... The idea settled in his mind.

As there was to be a regular influx of visitors to Harbourtown, why not support the local community by offering the tours? Caitlin could point out the areas of beauty they were privileged to see every day, pepper the talks with local history and perhaps even some pirate folklore - because that's what people thought of first when they saw the rocky shores in this area - and the bird life.

Ornithology from the university at Falmouth could verify the status of the area as one of the best, or so Yves hoped, and help build momentum for the tours. The more he thought about it, the more excited he became.

The Anchorage cousins too could benefit from his scheme - weaving stays in their accommodations with the Harbourtown tours, especially for those who wished to extend their time on the islands.

Yes, there was much to discuss, and arrange...

Chapter 3

Being an island with no mainland access by road, it was imperative that everyone on Harbourtown had a boat - be that a hired one or their own. The Treduggan family had their own boat, the large Kernow Star, which was well known to the islanders and frequently sighted on local pleasure trips.

As well as the few boats available in the harbour for hire - all given typical Cornish names; Seaton, Mermaid, Angarrack and Stithians, (although Mermaid may be atypical) - the Anchorage cousins over at Roundhouse had the boat named Tidehopper on permanent loan. Yves had Caitlin hire Stithians as the most suitable boat for excursions out to the smaller islands with the birders.

The Treduggan family were served by a local fisherman, Roger Shoal, and his boat, Fillet, knowing that any extra from his daily catch was sold on the mainland at Conning to the restaurants and the public houses. Very rarely was there a small haul from the surrounding waters, and so the idea that Roger's fish could be sold to diners at The Inn came quickly to fruition. Because of the anticipated increased demand, Roger was invited to find another fisherman with whom he could work, so as to not strain the supply into Conning.

It didn't take him long to select a young man to train, Nolan Keel. Nolan's boat was almost tellingly called The Storm. He was the youngest member of the Conning RNLI. Unlike most youngsters, he didn't mind the hard work and the early starts that came with the job, and began to carve himself a career out of fishing. Neither did he mind moving over to Harbourtown as part of the deal.

At first, Yves' idea of the hovercraft astounded a lot of the local people. Once they had seen the craft in action, they were won over; even more so when they learned that the RNLI had a fleet of hovercraft within their organisation. It was a natural connection to put boats with sea fayring, however nobody could argue that the hovercraft wasn't a safe and viable option.

It also allowed a larger cargo to be transferred to the mainland in one journey, as opposed to several of the necessarily smaller boats making more frequent journeys.

Oceanmaster was the main ferryboat/hovercraft named accordingly by Yves, who everyone knew had a sense of humour. His own boat had been renamed The Other Woman jokingly by Caitlin, as she said that he spent a lot of time out in it, scoping locations and coves, and bird sightings and patterns.

His time with The Other Woman grew as his new venture, he corrected himself - their new venture, began to take shape. Even Caitlin joined him for several hours worth of exploration as research into their new venture.

They regularly saw Lady Sybil with Walter waving cheerily at them and the Kernow Star cruising around with the Treduggan family and their adopted son, Kim Oke. Many rumours around the village, Harbourtown was classed as a village technically because of its small population, claimed that Kim was a bit of an oddball. However, their encounters with him had been nothing but pleasant, so Yves and Caitlin dismissed the unfriendly jibes.

Learning of Roger's trainee, they wondered if Kim would be the best person for Nolan to confide in and to learn the ropes, as such, of island life from. Caitlin was a matchmaker of sorts; she could put together a winning team from any group of individuals, moulding even the most stubborn into team players.

Another man she had on her radar, she laughed inwardly at the terrible pun, was the new local doctor, Quentin. Dr Quentin Farma was a decade senior to Kim and Nolan, she guessed. He had moved to Conning for the quieter life, or so it was said.

It wasn't long before the rumour mills discovered why he left Bude after living his whole life there. He was a heartbroken soul, having lost his first wife to a fatal illness, his second to a freak accident and a mere few months ago, his third prospective wife had left him at the altar.

It was a damn shame that Quentin had sworn off all women and condemned himself to bachelorhood, Caitlin thought. There would be new faces arriving at Harbourtown and new chances for romance and friendship. That was a given, not a casual observation.

Their harbourmaster Oxander Knowe was a local man, also working the important job of the lighthouse keeper. It made sense for both positions to be amalgamated as Harbourtown didn't need a full time harbourmaster due to its small size.

The general feeling was that Oxander ran the place well, juggling the two vital jobs with calm efficiency - no ships were wrecked, no near misses were logged, no cargo went astray: everything flowed smoothly. His schedule was a full one, but that didn't stop him flirting with the Anchorage cousins where possible. He was definitely a lady's man.

Caitlin nodded with her thoughts, Nolan would be better under Kim's wing than Oxander's, although everyone crossed paths on a regular basis. She couldn't be everywhere at once, and after all, it was possible that Nolan wouldn't need any prompting or another kind of intervention.

However, time would tell. It always did.

Chapter 4

If anyone should ask what a harbourmaster did, Oxander would launch into his memorised speech of what his responsibilities were.

Ports and harbours are busy places that can be hazardous. The main responsibility was the safety of everyone concerned - people living and working in or close to the harbour or port, the staff, customers and visitors. Therefore, harbourmasters must be familiar with all relevant safety, environmental and health laws at international, national and local level.

Port Marine Operations, Ship Arrival and Stay, Port Management, Strategic Planning Process, Other Authorities in the Port, Local Community, and Leisure Use of Ports are all summaries of the varied other tasks.

Recreational fisherman, diving clubs, rowing clubs, tour boat operators, visiting yachtsmen and power boat drivers, marina operators and many more must all be consulted as conflict may arise between those pursuing different activities within the area. The harbourmaster has an important role in engaging with interest groups, resolving any issues that arise and ensuring the safety of all harbour users.

Leisure activities take many forms, including recreational boating (both power and sail), swimming, diving and organised aquatic events. Harbourmasters can mitigate the risks associated with large aquatic events through the application of safety management principles and risk assessment. However, private and irregular use of the port is difficult to monitor and to control. Many ports and harbours use their websites and social media to promulgate safety information to port users. Another ongoing role.

Activity zoning as necessary to separate users, for

example keeping swimmers from personal watercraft, may be introduced. Prohibiting access to some areas may be required and will require local regulation. The focus for everyone should be on community engagement and finding harmonious methods for the co-existence of recreational activities. Any harbourmaster must decide on the set of rules for his/her area, and ensure that all users follow the stipulated regulations and legislations.

- Largely, he stopped there. Usually, he'd lost his listener's attention before now: their eyes glazed over with the bombardment of information and they just nodded dumbly. Not many asked him then what extra responsibility came with being the lighthouse keeper. If they did, he counted out the four main responsibilities on his fingers as he spoke.

"1. Playing tour guide. Lighthouses are historical landmarks, and many include a gift shop and/ or museum. Some have guided tours on their itinerary, and if you're living at one, as lighthouse keeper you're the guide, whether you like it or not.

2. Generating your own electricity. Each lighthouse needs somebody to turn on the light and the electricity too. Many are in remote locations or on islands, meaning a generator is often the only available power supply. Some lighthouses have no power at all (at least for keepers' quarters), and very few have cable or Wi-Fi. It is by no means a luxurious or glamorous lifestyle, despite what people may think.

3. Be prepared to survive alone. Lighthouses are intentionally remote outposts, often far from society, or located on islands. Some are far enough from civilization that they require a survivalist's ability to find drinkable water, store supplies, and go days without outside contact during

inclement weather.

4. Perform light keeping duties, no matter what. Finally, and perhaps most importantly, each keeper has a responsibility to ensure the lighthouse runs. Raising the flag first thing in the morning, turning on the generator and checking everything is functional. Some listen to Marine Radio after that. The day is free except for lighthouse repairs, maintenance, and tours. At night there's more to do, dealing with the flashing light and frequent fog horn alerts.

God forbid when a storm hits, the job is even worse!" Oxander usually finished.

Any inquisitive soul who hadn't been lost in the narrative would usually have their mouth hanging open by now. Oxander would exchange goodbyes with them as he walked towards the lighthouse, a perfect escape made. He lived there because it meant peace and quiet, relatively speaking, and it was a great vantage point to watch the harbour from. He could have chosen to live in the quarters beside the Harbourmaster's Office on the quay, opposite the lighthouse. Again it was a small, impersonal place - of the two, he chose Felix.

But he wasn't completely alone since the cat had made himself at home there also. Despite shooing the creature out several times, it kept returning. Since Oxander had allowed the cat to stay however, there had been no sign of any of the former rodent inhabitants. As far as Oxander was concerned, it had earned its keep. He knew others in Harbourtown were feeding it and often saw it around, patrolling and exploring. When he heard what they had named the animal, he laughed. Likewise, he adopted the name for the cat and sometimes was met with a frosty reception in the form of the narrowing of its eyes - they had come to an amicable acquaintance having the same home over time.

Chapter 5

Alicia Cakebread was born to be in the catering industry, as she felt her partner, Eddie, was also. Eddie Clare had the best bakery in Conning, in fact people visited from neighbouring towns such was his reputation. Running the bakery kitchen and shop was too much for one person, so he had been forced to employ a member of staff.

Any entrepreneur will tell you that the key to the success of their business is keeping costs low in order to maximise the profits. Eddie needed someone who would not only assist him but provide an asset to the business - enter cake queen, Alicia. She had all of the necessary qualifications and certain fetching qualities - bright and bubbly with customers and with suppliers; she drove a hard bargain to minimise the rising costs associated with the growing business.

Eddie began to fall in love with her charm and natural beauty - she was a true country girl, with a down to earth attitude. He knew that he had chosen well as a business partner and found himself wondering what it would be like to be partners outside of work... It didn't take long for their relationship to develop.

Four months later, disaster struck. When he was given the devastating news that the bakery had burnt down one night, Eddie turned to Alicia for comfort. Recalling how she gave words of wisdom readily, dishing out friendly reassurance and kindness alongside home baked goods to their clients, he felt the same benefits as she assured him that something else would come along. The secret to getting back into business was to stick with Alicia, he knew.

Fortunately, the policeman filing the report of arson on the row of buildings was Walter Copper. He knew of the

Treduggan family's plans but had secretly doubted their ability to recruit people to live there above their businesses. Most would say that the frequent trips to the mainland meant that it would not be necessary to stay: but it would make sense for someone to remain on the premises 24/7/365 for many reasons.

Suddenly he had the perfect candidates in front of him - but would they be right for the Inn? It was a huge jump from running a bakery to an Inn; a café would be a more appropriate move, he reasoned. He smiled then, recalling that the Treduggan family wanted both a café and an Inn. The plan was sure to come together, especially if he engineered it.

Shona Tate ran Conning's gift shop with her younger step-sister, Ursula. It was situated next door but one to the bakery; and sadly also destroyed in the arson attack that night. The two women were offered a relocation the very next day and agreed to view it.

Finding it beside the local pub was less than ideal, Shona frowned; her frown deepening when she measured the space, discovering that it ran only to half the square footage of their previous place. They would easily get in each other's way and tempers would fray, she foresaw.

Ursula was nothing but positive about it. They were in the best available location so they needed to make it work. Somehow.

Sighing, Shona knew she had no alternative but to agree - there were no other available sites within Conning's main parade, and they needed the guaranteed footfall of passing trade in order to make the business a continuing success.

Now they needed a rapid turnaround to get the place

ready to open as soon as possible. There would be a lot of work redesigning the area to fit in what was required... She sighed again.

David Tale and Tanya Hirst had been married for twenty three years despite not sharing the same surname. They ran Conning's popular public house which was endearingly called The Empty Tankard, with their son, Isaac, and his partner, Cecillia Saw. Isaac and Cecillia, or Cecil as she preferred to be known, were newlyweds.

David and Tanya were plotting their next move so as to give Isaac his own business now that he was married and had found his feet. Not that they would stop working, they were looking into other ventures as at 58 and 57 respectively they considered themselves too young to retire yet.

The four offered to help Shona and Ursula to 'make over' the new smaller shop, and became firm friends whilst doing so. They weren't the only regular visitors to the new premises - Walter's beat took him through the town at least twice a day. Remarkably, he always had time to look in on them, admire their progress, pass on some titbit of news he'd heard and partake of a cuppa before heading off again.

They grew more than used to seeing him; in fact, they both looked forward to the policeman's attention. Shona was hurt to see Ursula flirting with him - Walter was her age and therefore she was much more of a match for the older man than Ursula would ever be - and reprimanded her for her shameful behaviour.

Ursula laughed it off while Shona seethed. And that wasn't the only thing that annoyed Shona. Everything she touched, Ursula came along later and moved, just to spite her. The first, second, third and even fourth time, Shona bit her tongue. Some of the time what Ursula had changed made sense, so Shona let it go. Or at least tried to.

Paying more attention to her appearance now the shop was finished and ready to open to the public, Shona unleashed her charms on anyone who came through the door - including Walter, who wasn't going to argue if two lovely ladies decided they wanted to spoil him. To be fair, no man would.

Ursula remained a shameless flirt whenever a male customer arrived, even to the point where other customers noticed and began talking about the disrespectfulness of it. Shona's reputation was beginning to get a little smeary around the edges, but it had nothing to do with her...

Chapter 6

After the close of business, usually the two women had dinner together before heading their separate ways at home. Ursula hadn't only been let into Shona's place of work, she'd also been welcomed without question into her home.

Shona hadn't verbally shown her angst at having her privacy invaded by her step-sister. Merely she had made space in the second bedroom to accommodate Ursula's possessions - she had arrived with 4 bags!! - and promised to move more things soon so as to give her more space. To her credit, Ursula hadn't complained too loudly.

Ursula had always been a spoiled kid and had gotten away with far too much, in Shona's opinion. Her adulthood had taught her some wisdom and manners it seemed, as she had arrived on Shona's shop doorstep to plead with her to take her in, trembling and white as a sheet, and not just from the biting winter wind this far south.

That had been almost two years ago now: slowly, only now that she actually thought about it, maybe it hadn't been slowly at all, Ursula had taken more than she gave from the sibling relationship.

Despite Shona's rota dividing the household chores between them, Ursula did as little as possible. At the shop, she also did minimal work, and whilst it was true that her persuasive nature meant that she probably could have sold sand to the Arabs, she didn't pull her weight there either. She did what she wanted and at the times that suited her; no more, no less.

Shona's turn to cook meant that they'd get a decent meal: Ursula had taken to protesting that she was too tired to cook in the last few weeks. Although feeling it much more than her younger step-sister, they were both dog tired from trying to prepare the shop for opening as soon as humanly possible, Shona usually caved in and cooked anyway.

Tonight's schedule took the same nosedive - Ursula harrumphed and yawned and stretched and harrumphed some more.

"I'm beat," she declared.

Her earlier anger came back to Shona as the red mist descended. "I am beyond exhausted, you don't pull your weight anywhere!"

Ursula frowned. "I make more sales in one day than you make all week!"

That had been the wrong thing to say, she saw as Shona leant menacingly towards her, her expression darkening. Ursula felt a stab of fear. A flashback hit her: when the old shop had been ruined and they were offered the new premises, Shona had had to sell her home further inland in order to pay the substantial deposit.

Ursula hadn't known that was part of the deal when she'd so positively agreed with the idea of the new premises; she watched as Shona signed the papers and they both had to move out - and into the smaller accommodation above the new shop, beside the pub. It was a lot noisier and cramped here; still with two bedrooms but a smaller kitchen and bathroom, and a much smaller lounge, with of course zero outside space. Yet Shona hadn't uttered one word of disdain - not that Ursula had heard, anyway.

"You should watch what you say." Shona hissed, attempting to rein in her temper before their conversation became an argument.

"Oh yeah," Ursula smiled a wicked, teasing smile. "Like you would do anything about it. You hate confrontation. You'd rather bow to pressure than upset someone."

Shona knew then the truth in the old saying: the truth

hurts. Yes, she didn't like confrontation and hated arguing, but there was nothing wrong with that. More often than not any mistakes were simply rectified. Nobody was perfect, and you got nowhere in life beating up yourself - or those around you.

Why Ursula was using her good nature against her, she didn't know. Managing to make her way out of the room without exploding, she tossed the words over her shoulder.

"Make your own dinner."

Ursula's mouth dropped open, and her smug expression vanished.

Shona headed to the pub next door to seek solace in Tanya.

She had become her first and best friend in Conning years ago when Shona had sought her new life in the small coastal town. Their bond strengthened with the milestone events in their lives - Shona's successful business venture with the gift shop; the pub being named the best in Cornwall - a truly high accolade; Ursula's sudden arrival and, more recently, the wedding of Issac and Cecillia.

Tanya had often spoken with her about hers and David's ideas, finding her a decent sounding board - Shona sometimes thought of things that neither of them had. In their back room - Shona laughed when they referred to the space as this, because it was three times as large as her previous premises, six times as large now she thought to herself sorrowfully - Tanya poured them out a glass each from the pre-chilled bottle of wine while she prepared a meal for herself, David and their guest.

It spoke volumes for the thoughtfulness of the pub's patrons that they knew the owners liked a quiet hour between 7 pm and 8 pm, and mostly held fire on their rounds. At times, they even delayed their arrival to coincide with 8 pm.

To show their gratitude, David declared that 8 pm signified Happy Hour, meaning drinks were half price. As a rule The Empty Tankard public house served their last round at 10.30, so that by the 11 pm closing time there weren't many, if any, stragglers to kick out.

Shona considered their latest plan very well thought out. The Treduggan family wanted to hire David and Tanya for the Inn, recognising their experience and reputation. Isaac and his new bride could easily run The Empty Tankard, and if it was at all necessary, either David or Tanya could journey back and forth to the mainland. It remained to be seen what would happen in the High Season - the summer months of July and August, and that was their only sticking point. Tanya watched her friend's expression with interest.

"I'm sure," Shona began, "you'd find lots of help around. I wouldn't mind having to do a few shifts if necessary. It's not like I have to come far." A wry smile crossed her lips. "Such a shame you don't have an Ursula to help you," she snorted, "but someone of more use."

Tanya winced, and laughed. "I'm not sure how much I'd trust Ursula behind the pumps."

Shona too laughed. "You could put her in charge of the dishwasher."

They both cackled at the idea.

Chapter 7

Being new to the business of renovation, the Treduggans had no idea how much space their joint ideas would take up. Not that this was an issue as everything on Harbourtown Island was theirs.

When it was clear that the footprints of both the Inn and the café left some space needing to be filled, they had another idea: a gift shop selling locally made produce. It could attach to the café and Inn, linking the two premises not just physically by location between the two, but also with the stock being used by both businesses and sold to visitors.

This would prove a shrewd business move.

Alicia and Eddie were offered the café once the Treduggans heard of the burnt down bakery and were reassured that it was the fault of an arsonist - not the owner, or his help.

Now that the insurance had paid out on the ruined bakery on the mainland, Eddie was thrilled to be offered the opportunity; unabashed by the idea that he must live on the premises.

He had been wondering where he could set up his new business, having not put much faith in Walter's 'grand plan' of selling them to the Treduggans. Pleasantly surprised that it had worked out, he pondered his next step. Naturally it made sense to ask Alicia to help him with the new business - and move in with him.

Caught up with the excitement of it all, Alicia agreed. Declaring that she has dreamt of something like this for years, Eddie's smile widened. The idea of marriage had been on his mind for a while since they had met, but he didn't want to rush, knowing exactly the right time and place for the engagement would come along at the right moment.

He decided, nonetheless, to rent out his flat in Conning. After six months, they would be able to determine whether or not the cafe was a viable option both for work and living: after this time he could continue to rent or sell. Alicia was flat sharing with two friends, so didn't have the same quandary - moving on was far easier for her.

Yves agreed to the rather brilliant idea put forward by the Head of the Ornithological department - he needed to double check if that was the right title for the man before he arrived - during their most recent email communication. The first, and unofficial, birding group should be a selection from their fellow enthusiasts.

Both he and Caitlin could learn a lot from the experiment: increasing their knowledge, learning how to structure the birders tour and giving it a trial run before being let loose on the paying public. Likely there would be more than one expedition, the email hinted, and visitors were almost guaranteed to return. A shiver of excitement went through him - Caitlin reacted the same when she read the words.

Harbourtown Inn, Harbourtown Café and in the middle, Harbourtown Gift Shop, were primed and ready to go - the grand opening was earmarked for the Easter long weekend, just around the corner in the calendar. Word spread fast.

The Anchorage cousins were eager to get on board with the plans, and set about preparing their business for a collaboration. Each business networked extensively so as to maximise the potential revenue from the expansion of Harbourtown. Opportunities like this didn't come along often.

Chapter 8

Internet searches confirmed what the Head Ornithologist had told them - this part of the Cornish coast boasted a huge bird population. Some of the more common species they all recognised: even the self proclaimed 'townies' of Conning knew the difference between a black headed gull and an Arctic Tern.

In passing someone collectively referred to the seagulls, rather vulgarly, as shite-hawks. Although it was an apt description, it was not one that would fit in with the sophistication of the tour!

Lapwing, snipe, curlew, raven, falcons, swallow, razorbill, shelduck, teal, mallards, herons, bitterns, pigeons, thrushes, finches, partridges, owls, buntings, various geese, grebe, cormorants, rooks, gannets, swans, woodpeckers, chaughs, jays, jackdaws, tits, pipits, house martins and sand martins, nuthatch and treecreeper - and many birds of prey.

The list of sightings in the area seemed inexhaustible!

Yves made a special note of the local Ornithologist legends, and various birding websites that could be of use to them in the near future. Even social media postings by Cornwall Birding fanatics were valuable information, he realised.

The idea that rarer birds were seen in the area when blown off course was highlighted by certain names - the American Belted kingfisher had last been seen decades ago in the 1980s. It would be too much to hope that someone on one of the early tours would spot something very rare... but it was possible!

Working out the format of the tour was surprisingly straightforward.

A break at the café after walking around part of Harbourtown Island and a tour of the gardens belonging to the Treduggan family that Caitlin tended would be the first part. Tide timings and seal sightings in harbour would play a vital role in the next part - out in the boat to the islands. It had to be the boat not the hovercraft, although Caitlin allowed herself to indulge in the thought that the birds might get used to the noise of the craft and, not before long, ignore it. That was a little too much to hope for, or so she thought...

Before they allowed anyone to leave, at least one of the cousins from Roundhouse gave a presentation to tell visitors about the vacations they offered. As a finale, David and Tanya sent them to The Empty Tankard on the mainland before they all dispersed home.

And then, the day was here.

When the Ornithologists arrived, there were thirty of them. Caitlin was shocked by such a large number and calculated it would require two boats to take them all out on the tour, thankful that Yves was available to help. This also taught them to limit future tours to 15 people as she couldn't always rely on her partner being available.

Yves, struck by the notion that they arrived in a flock, managed to contain his mirth, sure that nobody would laugh with him. The Head of the Ornithological Department he had been in communication with turned out to actually be a woman, all along he thought it was a man using the name Les. Although he was surprised, Caitlin wasn't and easily engaged her in conversation, discovering she was a mine of great ideas.

Talking excitedly amongst themselves, Yves and Caitlin steered the visiting Ornithologists into Harbourtown Inn for a drink to celebrate the success of their opening day of the new venture. The weather had been perfect, the water calm, the birds flittered back and forth regularly. If they could have engineered it, they couldn't have produced a better tour.

All talk stopped when Vimto strolled in as usual and plonked himself down by the fire. At the flick of a switch the real-looking fire could produce warmth, and it drew people towards it as if it was real.

Situated in the middle of the room, technically as it was against a partial wall, it meant that Vimto was the centre of attention. He could now get through the wooden door, nosing and pawing at the right place to push it open enough to squeeze through.

Caitlin laughed, keen to reassure her patrons that there was no issue with the animal. "Don't worry about him, he's friendly to everyone, that's Vimto. He lives in the lighthouse." Yves laughed too. "Most people confuse Felix and Vimto when they hear about them - Felix is the lighthouse, not the cat."

"Vimto?" Someone questioned. "As in the juice?"

Caitlin nodded. "The local kids christened him. He's of mixed breeding and has two different coloured eyes."

"Really?" Several of their distinguished guests were amazed by this, and a few got to their feet to wander over to the cat.

Vimto looked up at the approaching humans curiously: friend or foe was the first decision he had to make towards any human. Strangers were more difficult to guess correctly...

Chapter 9

Arranging a grand opening preview tour day had been a genius idea. Yves and Caitlin arranged three tour slots per day - morning, afternoon and early evening. This would allow them to judge if the limit they'd set per tour would work, as well as the timings.

9am until 11am. 12.30 until 2.30pm. 4pm until 6pm. The timing worked out fine for most of the year, able to be easily adjusted to the shorter days of winter - and the different tide timings - to 10am until 12 noon and 1pm until 3pm.

Caitlin wondered about having longer tours that would focus on more time for bird watching, but initially they kept to the arranged timetable. In time, they would be able to tell what worked and what needed tweaking.

By having the café offerings on each scheduled break as a cold selection, it not only helped food preparations, but allowed a 2 hour timetable instead of necessitating 3 hours to include a longer stop.

Plus, the visitors could partake in a discounted meal offer with either the Inn at Harbourtown or Conning's pub The Empty Tankard. Anyone who had been out in the boat for a while when it was cold and/or damp would welcome hot food and drink; by enticing them with a discount, David and Tanya hoped at one establishment or the other to increase the revenue from the birder tourists.

Everyone referred to them as the birder tourists, or birders; lots of local wildlife meant that visitors would be guaranteed sightings of Cornwall's animal life.

This was what hook the Anchorage cousins were using. Take advantage of a discounted rate for lessons of painting or a photography day session at Roundhouse for any tour visitor. Multiple lesson or stay discounts were offered to tempt people to return, whether or not they were a birder. This was their special offer idea for the grand opening; extended to include anyone undertaking the previous day's tours.

By the Friday of the weekend - technically two days into the opening - Tanya couldn't run the Inn and the Gift Shop by herself; likewise, Eddie and Alicia were too busy to lend a hand in both the café and the shop. Actioning the back up plan made with Shona and Ursula, Yves picked up Ursula en route to dropping off the previous passengers and collecting another group.

Shona had to admit that she was jealous to miss out on all the excitement, but it was a relief to be rid of Ursula from under her feet. She began to daydream the arrangement would be a permanent one...

After the success of the grand opening, and a steady influx of casual visitors and birders to Harbourtown, Tanya offered Ursula the permanent position of running the shop. Knowing that Shona is becoming increasingly frustrated with their living and working situation, it was also in the back of her mind that Eddie and Alicia would be able to help Ursula out, while leaving herself and David free, if necessary, to switch back across to The Empty Tankard on Conning. It was an arrangement that would work well for all concerned, she thought.

Shona's words - "You should remember I helped you when nobody else would!" - echoed around Ursula's mind as she thought over the offer from Tanya. As far as she could see it was win-win.

Shona already knew what was happening, having given

Tanya her permission, as technically Ursula was her member of staff - and her responsibility. Tanya knew the conversation between them all had to be kept business-like; smiling at Shona's obvious relief of the situation.

For the first few weeks, Ursula travelled back and forth every day. Her temperament improved somewhat as time passed - Shona didn't question it, but was sceptical of its permanence.

The Conning shop was easily managed alone now it was much smaller. Regular trade thankfully hadn't been affected by the opening of the Harbourtown store. There was, however, one reason to still resent Ursula.

When she moved across to work in Harbourtown, Walter no longer made it part of his routine to stop off at the shop. Shona was heartbroken by his absence - he had seemed to enjoy spending time with her, what had changed?

Everything froze in that moment as the truth slapped her hard. He hadn't been spending time with her, he'd been spending time with Ursula and her. His absence confirmed that he wasn't interested in Shona. Tanya confirmed that Walter was indeed a regular guest at the store, and at the Inn and at the café; in fact he spent more of his time on Harbourtown Island than ever before.

Extremely hurt by this rebuff, her feelings stamped over and trodden into submission, Shona realised that she had been unwittingly involved in a love triangle! Love truly was blind!

If that was how it was going to be, then there was nothing she could do about it. She knew she needed to follow common sense and not get caught up in her tangled emotions.

However! It seemed that Ursula's special skill of pushing

Shona's buttons was in force - and it didn't take long until she flipped. Angrily, she tossed Ursula's belongings out with her, telling her to move to Harbourtown permanently if it was so much better and so much lovelier and had everything and everyone she needed. Despite her anger, she managed to mimic Ursula's voice perfectly.

Thrown by this out of character behaviour by her step-sister, Ursula shrugged as she left for the evening hovercraft journey back over to Harbourtown. Tanya had told her that she could move into the accommodation above, beside her and David, when she agreed to take the job permanently, so she knew she had somewhere to stay and wasn't worried about being kicked out of Shona's place. She could however play on it to gain more attention…

Chapter 10

"Ain't very sisterly, that. If you ask me."
Ursula nodded at the man's statement.

"Just as well you had somewhere else to go." Another man put in.

Enthused Ursula nodded again, her expression turned sombre. "I had no idea she could be so cruel." She mumbled, but loud enough to make sure that she could be heard. "I'm so grateful that Harbourtown rescued me."
The others rolled their eyes silently.

"The only rescuing we do around here is at sea." One voice arose from the crowd.

Despite scanning the crowd, Ursula couldn't pick out the speaker. "I was rescued, I don't care what you say." The frown turned her face sour.

"I was rescued once," a man in the corner spoke. He'd had a few beers that evening and had become unusually talkative. "Towednack comin' outta the black storm was a vision!"

Ursula's frown deepened. "Toad-neck? Who on Earth has such a silly name?"
Most of the assembled crowd groaned.

"Proves she's a true blonde," someone laughed.

"Towednack." Oxander approached the bar for a refill, standing beside Ursula's occupied bar stool. He corrected her gently. "You can't have lived here long if you don't know about the Inshore Lifeboat."

Ursula looked up into his dark, brooding eyes and immediately was tongue tied.

"Well?" He prompted, giving her a warm smile.

Ursula shrugged and rediscovered her womanly wiles. "Maybe not. Tell me more." She pulled out another bar stool and patted the seat invitingly. "I'm sure we haven't met..."

Their exchange was interrupted by the arrival of Vimto, or rather someone's shout of the fact that he had arrived.

"Oxander, your cat's here. He'll be wantin' a drink too no doubt." Someone called out, much to the crowd's pleasure. The roar that went up drowned out every conversation in the place. Meanwhile, Vimto had spotted Oxander and held his stare from across the room.

"Cats don't drink beer!" Ursula exclaimed.

"Sure they do." The drinker nearest Vimto put down his half finished half pint.

The Inn's patrons collectively held their breath as the cat moved closer and sniffed, wrinkling his multicolour face. Tentatively he pawed the glass and then stopped, looking up at the previous owner.

"It's Salty Sea Dawg, the local brew." He said, as if to answer the unspoken question.

"Aye, it's good stuff." His drinking companion encouraged. Vimto inclined his head as if to accept this, and without any further ado bent his neck to take a taster.

Silence fell as the sound of slurping grew louder as the glass emptied. Straightening up, Vimto's eyes widened and he burped noisily. The place erupted in fits of laughter.

"He has the most amazing eyes!" Ursula declared as Vimto sauntered towards them, and unsteadily jumped up onto the bar beside her.

Shoving his bum in her face and waving his tail around, as cats have a tendency to do, he delighted in her attention as she made a fuss over him.

"Not a graceful beast." Oxander said half under his breath.

"Don't call him a beast! He's beautiful! I wish he were mine." Ursula's voice became wistful and dreamy. "I never had a cat, but I always wanted one."

"You don't own a cat, it owns you." Tanya said, reaching out to scratch Vimto behind the ears.

"Ain't that the truth!" A few voices agreed.

Moving delicately across the bar, Vimto sniffed at pint glasses, causing several drinkers to cover their glasses and take them off the counter out of reach. Lots of laughter followed this.

"Watch it, don't get him hooked, he can't buy a round!" A voice from the back of the room joked.

The usual bar staple of black olives in a dish on the counter caught Vimto's attention. He sniffed at them, pawing one out of the dish and onto the counter. Before anyone could move to take it from him, he'd eaten it.

Surprised gasps arose.

"Cats aren't allowed human food, are they?"

"How did he do that?"

"Will it poison him, d'you think?"

Smiling - if it was possible for a cat to smile, opinion differed - Vimto hooked around the dish and produced another black olive, devouring that also. Sniffing at the dish again, aware that everyone was watching to see how many he would eat, Vimto held his head high and walked away from it. His audience laughed, some with relief. Sticking his head in an open crisp packet next, he crunched delightedly at what was on offer.

"Oi!" Exclaimed the owner of the crisps. "Bugger off. Get yer own!" Snatching the bag away, the man found himself in Vimto's gaze - he disappeared with his crisps and his pint. He had also been one of those who had rescued his drink from Vimto's questing nose a few moments ago.

Half shrugging, Vimto flopped onto his side, sprawling over the counter and fell asleep. Some would later swear he was snoring like a drunkard.

Chapter 11

Animals make the best companions; it was agreed wholeheartedly by the people of Conning and the surrounding islands once the story had spread. Ursula had been delighted by her encounter with Vimto, and his human, Oxander. She hadn't been the only one - Vimto's antics soon spread beyond the mainland, catching everyone's humour.

Isaac and his father, David, weren't sure what to think; Cecillia was sure it was against trading standards; Tanya laughed and joked about setting up an exclusive menu for the famous feline. A bad taste joke became a catchphrase of sorts - enjoy creature comforts at the Inn and you'll come out feline good.

Felix and Vimto were the best features of the island, someone joked darkly. That was a true conversation stopper.

What an unusual name, and he certainly was an unusual man, Ursula couldn't get the mysterious Oxander out of her mind. Why had they not met before?

In Conning she had met lots of people - and gained lots of admirers, but none were as appealing as him. Was it purely because she knew very little about him? Or was it his cat that did it for her? She wasn't sure. Maybe a combination of both?

Asking around, she learned that he was harbourmaster and lighthouse keeper - that explained why they'd never met before; Oxander didn't get much in the way of free time and certainly hardly ever enough to get out for a drink. Learning that he, and Vimto, lived in the lighthouse she was astonished.

It seemed a romantic idyll, she mused aloud to Tanya

later on that day. Tanya set her straight, informing her of the responsibilities of lighthouse living and the required sacrifices it entailed. She was stunned, but the idea blossomed in her mind that she could use this to her advantage. Whenever she wanted to see him, she knew exactly where he would be. She grinned.

Packing cat food and Prosecco the next night, she began the long walk along the slippery cobbles of the harbour dock. The lighthouse could be seen wherever you were on Harbourtown, its bright beam lit up everything in its path. That was fine by her, it meant she had her own personal spotlight, or as near as.

Giggling with the thought, she almost missed Oxander rushing out of the lighthouse and disappearing down the opposite path a long way ahead of her. Try as she might, she couldn't catch up with him: at the place where he'd disappeared, the light was blocked out by the trees.

The stillness of the night was broken by the sound of the lifeboat engine as Towednack motored beyond the harbour walls before vanishing. She could make out three figures standing on the deck, or whatever it was called, but that was all.

At the lighthouse, the door was ajar she was alarmed to see. Then it struck her: nobody would be coming here to rob or ransack the lighthouse. It didn't feel right to enter the building without him, as much as she wanted to wait for him. In the rapidly approaching darkness, she left a quick scribbled note on top of the bag she'd brought, placing both on the stairwell between the first and second flight of steps so it would be sheltered and also easy for him to find.

'Hoped we could share this and get to know each other, and something to distract your cat too. Another time! Ursula (the cute blonde at the Inn) x '

45

Over an hour later Yves, Oxander and Nolan returned from their after dark practice exercise - Nolan's first at Harbourtown. Roger had induced him ten days ago, and it had shamefully taken this long to get the three men together.

With Oxander and Yves as the best candidates to upskill Nolan, they needed to train him up fast - RNLI rules state that crews should train together every week, at sea and ashore.

Such training exercises focused on teamwork, technical competence and safe operating procedures - covering everything from boat-handling, search and rescue, and navigation, to radar training, radio communications and casualty care. Planned rescue scenarios involving other emergency services such as the Coastguard and fire and rescue services should occur every so often so that in an emergency, everyone knows what to do and what should happen.

While they were out, they tested Nolan, sure that he was competent but nonetheless it did no harm to check his knowledge.

"Training first." Yves began.

Nolan took a deep breath before beginning. "Every crew member follows a structured programme of competence-based training and assessment: an agreed range of skills and competencies necessary to complete particular tasks. They also undertake operational training, designed to help meet required fitness standards. Crew training is continuous and learning never stops."

Both Yves and Oxander nodded. "Good." They both said and smiled.

"Roger told you about our members' roles and

responsibilities when he showed you around the boat?" Oxander checked.

Nolan nodded. "You are the mechanic," he looked at Yves, "but also the coxswain." He turned to Oxander. "You are the helm, or commander. That makes sense, in light of your duties on land."

Oxander nodded.

"Quentin, Roger and Walter are the other crew members."

"Excellent." Yves beamed at him. "How long did you spend looking over Towednack?"

Nolan frowned. "About an hour, I think. By the time Roger showed me the protective gear, the overall boat and where things were, what the dials each mean, what screen to watch the most and then we went over rope work. As we are an inshore lifeboat, it needs only three of us before we can launch."

Both Oxander and Yves were nodding.

"Our medical adviser must be Quentin?" He asked, receiving another two nods.

"You probably won't be surprised to learn that I am the lifeboat operations manager and press officer." Oxander informed him.

"That again makes sense." Nolan nodded.

"After how long did they send you to Poole for training?" Oxander wondered aloud.

"Six months exactly, but we went up to Mousehole or Sennen for regular training by one of the mobiles in a group - from Sennen, St Ives, Newlyn and Mousehole." Nolan smiled. "It made sense in many ways." He added when he saw their surprised expressions.

They both nodded.

"Has Roger told you that I am responsible for the local educational talks?" Yves asked.

Nolan nodded. "It's important to explain the risks to people who don't know them and share our safety knowledge with everyone on the coast. Most people think that's the lifeguards' role, but there is some crossover I suspect."

Yves nodded, very pleased with how this was going. Soon they would be stopping at the planned spot to officially begin to get technical with the training, but there was time yet. "Do you know our local lifeguards?"

"Only by sight, I've never met them. By all accounts they do a fantastic job, the three of them."

"They sure do." Oxander agreed. "We're almost there. I want to go over navigation, radar and radio communications with you. Our next session will include casualty care with Quentin."

Nolan nodded, sharing a look with Yves as if to say 'he's very self important, isn't he?' - both of them tried not to laugh as they were thinking the same thing.

On their way back, Yves told him that next on the list of his training was the hovercraft; explaining that this was not kept in the harbour with the other boats; the mudflats on the south side of the Island were the ideal place to locate the vessel. Naturally, it was kept on a raised platform from the mudflats so as not to sustain damage.

Once Towednack was safely docked, the trio went their separate ways once more. It struck Yves then that Nolan could also be a second ferryman between Harbourtown, Conning and the other islands once he was trained.

He could also encourage the young man to engage with the mechanical maintenance alongside him: he smiled widely with the thought. Nolan was going to be a great boost to their team and to Harbourtown itself, he felt.

Nolan couldn't hide his grin at how the first expedition had gone. It was a relief that it had gone so well, and he had wanted to impress his new counterparts. Job done, he thought.

Oxander was not smiling. Having entered the lighthouse and strided out to mount the three dozen steps as always, his foot had connected with the bag half hidden in the dark, throwing him off balance.

Chapter 12

Having received the short SOS call from Oxander, Quentin soon arrived at Felix with his motorboat tethered in the harbour below the towering structure.

What he discovered inside the lighthouse shocked him. Blood up the stairs, up the wall, on the hand rail curving around the tight space of the stairwell... A huge gash had opened up on the side of Oxander's head, but his leg hurt the worst, he made sure to insist.

Accidents always happen in the most awkward of places, Quentin thought to himself. His casualty was between the first and second flights of stone steps in the lighthouse - a narrow, twisty, shadowed passageway. It was also cold, he noted as Oxander shivered and cried out in pain where his side also hit the stairwell.

Eyebrows knitted together as Oxander told him this, Quentin knew of the resistance he was about to receive but he had no choice in the matter - they needed external help. The rescue helicopter employed by the Coastguard was the only way to get Oxander to hospital.

Telling him such, he received a scathing look.

"I don't need to go to the hospital. I simply need your help to get up the rest of the stairs and carry on." He flinched as Quentin pressed a gauze pad to the side of his head, instructing him to hold onto it to stem the bleeding. As he did so, Quentin saw it immediately soaked through: he pressed another on top.

"Ow!" Oxander verbalised his complaint.

Pursing his lips, Quentin pondered his next question. "You cannot put any weight on that leg?" He checked.

Oxander shook his head, but carefully. "I can't get up by myself, but if you..."

"How does it feel?" Quentin cut him off.

"Red hot pokers of pain." He shrugged. "But I can't leave my post."

Quentin actually laughed. This had the wrong effect on his patient.

"Don't stand there laughing, do something." Oxander demanded angrily.

"Oh, I will." Quentin turned around and made the call outside, returning once more to Oxander after a few minutes of conversation. "They are arranging for your replacement whilst we go to the hospital to check you over. I wouldn't be surprised if you have broken something." He frowned.

Knowing that Oxander was fit and strong, he suspected the injury was a serious one.

"You didn't hear anything crack, did you?"

"I don't really know." Oxander spoke quieter now, his whole demeanour shrunk somewhat. "My head, my side, everything together, it all happened so quickly; one minute I was on my feet, the next I wasn't."

Gravely Quentin nodded. "You did the right thing calling me, and I've done the right thing escalating your call for help. Don't worry, I won't let you go alone." He flashed him a smile. "In case any other demented woman tries to kill you."

Oxander smiled, wanting to laugh at the joke, but not at the same time, knowing it would hurt too much. The simple act of breathing hurt more than it should. He wanted to protest as Quentin unfurled the thermal blanket and threaded it around his shoulders, shivering again he wondered - as Quentin was - if he was reacting to the cold, or if it was shock.

With that thought, the situation hit him hard. Thank God Quentin had come quickly to his aid, what if he'd been left here for hours... Above the usual sound of the sea waves crashing against the harbour walls, they could now hear the helicopter as it came nearer.

Everyone in Conning and the surrounding islands heard the helicopter, able to follow its progress in the night sky because of the powerful lights onboard. From Conning it was difficult to tell quite where it was hovering over, but the residents of Harbourtown were shocked to see it was at the lighthouse on the end of the harbour.

Only the next morning did they find out the truth - Walter informed them of the news on his daily round: Quentin had taken Oxander to Penzance hospital in the rescue helicopter after a nasty accident in the lighthouse. Shock at the news spread throughout the village.

Yves and Caitlin were first to see Quentin later that day; shocked when he informed them that Oxander would be in hospital for a few days, and after that, he would recuperate at Quentin's place in neighbouring Bountiful Bay.

Reassuring them that duties had been taken over by a relief lighthouse keeper, Pierre Leviant, and that Oxander was in the best place, he told them briefly his version of events when they questioned him. Only there to retrieve some of Oxander's personal effects, he sidestepped their other questions.

Going straight to the Inn to find Ursula and the others, Yves and Caitlin gathered also Eddie and David and Tanya. Alicia was on the mainland sourcing supplies for the cafe and hadn't yet heard the news.

Together in the doorway of the shop between the deserted Inn and the cafe, Tanya slipped her arm around Ursula's shoulders as she began to cry as she realised Oxander's accident was her fault!

David reassuringly stated that it had been an accident

and she hadn't meant to cause him harm, everyone would see that. Ursula wallowed in his common sense, until she realised that everyone would blame her and turn against her. She wailed, the noise blocking out Tanya's and Eddie's likewise words of comfort.

They all looked at each other, more than lost for what to say.

Chapter 13

Ursula paused as she thought about it. "The lifeboat is here. But I saw a lifeboat station further along the coast?"

Pierre grimaced. "The nearest to here is the old lifeboat station at Penlee, the replacement is further along." He had joined the locals the next night at Harbourtown Inn to make himself known and cheer them up after the accident.

"Old?" Ursula repeated, confused. "Why keep an old one if there's a replacement?"

Pierre, being an outsider to this part of the world, had thought every coastal dwelling person knew the legend of Penlee, but he hadn't met Ursula.

He drew in a deep breath. "On the night of 19th December 1981, the local lifeboat Solomon Browne went to the aid of a stricken vessel called the Union Star, after an initial rescue attempt by helicopter failed. The volunteer crew of eight tackled hurricane force 12 winds in the storm, with waves of up to 60 feet. Nothing further was heard after they had radioed that they'd managed to get four on board. All sixteen people lost their lives that night."

Ursula kept a respectable silence for a minute before she questioned him. "The old one is kept as some kind of memorial?"

Pierre nodded. "They had a garden made there also. You should visit it sometime."

"If it was such bad weather, why did the lifeboat go out?" She saw his incredulous expression and continued. "They have a responsibility to save lives I know, but surely that was a suicide mission?"

Pierre winced. "It showed incredible bravery, granted. Whenever they get an emergency call, it is never ever thought of as a suicide mission. Lifeboats now are larger and faster; training is first class as is the equipment they use. Crews are brave, fearless volunteers who wish to uphold the traditions of the RNLI. Much like the fire brigade, the police and the ambulance service, they are emergency service personnel who put others before themselves."

Urusla nodded thoughtfully. "I need to do some research." She gave him a thankful smile.

That evening, she set out to find what she needed on the Internet.

'The Penlee lifeboat disaster occurred on 19 December 1981 off the coast of Cornwall. The lifeboat Solomon Browne, based at the Penlee Lifeboat Station near Mousehole, went to the aid of the vessel Union Star after its engines failed in heavy seas. After the lifeboat had rescued four people, both vessels were lost; in all, sixteen people died including eight volunteer lifeboatmen.

The MV Union Star was a mini-bulk carrier registered in Dublin, it sailed to IJmuiden in the Netherlands to collect a cargo of fertiliser for its maiden voyage to Arklow in Ireland. It was carrying a crew of five: Captain Henry Morton; Mate James Whittaker, Engineer George Sedgwick, Crewman Anghostino Verressimo, and Crewman Manuel Lopes. Also on board was the captain's family (his wife Dawn with teenage stepdaughters Sharon and Deanne) who had been picked up at an unauthorised call at Brightlingsea in Essex.

Near the south coast of Cornwall, 8 miles (13 km) east of the Wolf Rock, the new ship's engines failed. It was unable to restart them but did not make a mayday call. Assistance was offered by a tug, the Noord Holland, but Morton initially refused the offer, later accepting after consulting the ship's owners. Winds were gusting at up to 90 knots (100 mph; 170 km/h) – hurricane, force 12 – producing waves up to 60 feet (18 m) high. The powerless ship was blown across Mount's Bay towards the rocks of Boscawen Cove, near Lamorna.

As the ship was close to shore, the Coastguard at Falmouth summoned a Royal Navy Sea King helicopter from 820 Naval Air Squadron (who were providing cover for 771 Naval Air Squadron), RNAS Culdrose. It used the call sign "Rescue 80" during the mission. The aircraft crew were unable to winch anyone off the ship as the wind was too violent.

The Coastguard had difficulties contacting the secretary of the nearest lifeboat station, Penlee Lifeboat Station at Mousehole on the west side of the bay. They eventually contacted Coxswain Trevelyan Richards and asked him to put the lifeboat on standby in case the helicopter rescue failed. He summoned the lifeboat's volunteer crew and picked seven men to accompany him in the lifeboat.

They were Second Coxswain/Mechanic Stephen Madron, Assistant Mechanic Nigel Brockman, Emergency Mechanic John Blewett, and crewmembers Charlie Greenhaugh, Kevin Smith, Barrie Torrie and Gary Wallis. Neil Brockman, the son of Nigel Brockman, got to the lifeboat station on time, but was turned down for the trip by Trevelyan Richards, who was reluctant to take out two members of the same family that night.'

Ursula sucked her breath in sharply. Had Richards known they were on a mission that was likely to cause such devastation, or was it purely regulation?

'The lifeboat launched at 8:12 pm and headed out through the storm to the drifting coaster. The lifeboat was the

Solomon Browne, a wooden 47-foot (14 m) Watson-class boat built in 1960 and capable of 9 knots (17 km/h). After it had made several attempts to get alongside, four people managed to jump across; the captain's family and one of the men were apparently safe. The lifeboat radioed that 'we've got four off', but that was the last heard from either vessel.

Lt Cdr Smith USN, the pilot of the rescue helicopter, later reported that: The greatest act of courage that I have ever seen, and am ever likely to see, was the penultimate courage and dedication shown by the Penlee crew when it manoeuvred back alongside the stricken ship in over 60 ft breakers and rescued four people shortly after the Penlee had been bashed on top of it's hatch covers. They were truly the bravest eight men I've ever seen, who were also totally dedicated to upholding the highest standards of the RNLI.

Other lifeboats were summoned to try to help their colleagues from Penlee. The Sennen Cove Lifeboat found it impossible to make headway round Land's End. The Lizard Lifeboat found a serious hole in its hull when it finally returned to its slipway after a fruitless search.

In the aftermath of the disaster, wreckage from the Solomon Browne was found along the shore, and the Union Star lay capsized onto the rocks, west of Tater Du Lighthouse. Some, but not all, of the 16 bodies were eventually recovered.

The inquiry into the disaster determined that the loss of the Solomon Browne was: in consequence of the persistent and heroic endeavours by the coxswain and his crew to save the lives of all from the Union Star. Such heroism enhances the highest traditions of the Royal National Lifeboat Institution in whose service they gave their lives.

Coxswain Trevelyan Richards was posthumously awarded the Royal National Lifeboat Institution's gold medal, while the remainder of the crew were all posthumously awarded bronze medals. The station itself was awarded a gold medal service plaque.

The disaster prompted a massive public appeal for the benefit of the village of Mousehole which raised over £3 million (equivalent to £11.6 million in 2019), although there was an outcry when the government tried to tax the donations.

Two nights before the disaster, Charlie Greenhaugh, who in civilian life was the landlord of the Ship Inn on the quayside in Mousehole, had turned on the village's Christmas lights. After the storm, the lights were left off but three days later his widow Mary asked for them to be repaired and lit again.

The village has been lit up each December since then, but on the anniversary of the disaster they are turned off at 8:00 pm for an hour as an act of remembrance. A plaque was also erected on the Ship Inn on behalf of the tenants, managers, directors and employees of the St Austell Brewery, the pub's owner.

Within a day of the disaster enough people from Mousehole had volunteered to form a new lifeboat crew. In 1983 a new lifeboat station (still known as 'Penlee') was opened nearby at Newlyn where a faster, larger boat could be kept moored afloat in the harbour. Neil Brockman later became the coxswain of the station's Severn-class lifeboat.

The old boathouse at Penlee Point with its slipway is kept the same as it was when the lifeboat launched and a memorial garden was created beside it in 1985 to commemorate the crew of the Solomon Browne.'

Ursula could only imagine what the tragedy had done to the community. She was filled with admiration for the new recruits of the RNLI, aware then of the vital work they selflessly did. Nowadays she supposed the crews stood a better chance against the elements - the boats weren't wooden, for starters!

She wanted to find out more about the RNLI, and as the night was still young, she had time to do more searching within the ultimate resource of the Internet. Recalling then at home she'd once said that everything could be found on the Internet, her father had scoffed and declared that it wasn't so clever. She still didn't understand, but there was a lot she didn't understand about her family.

Chapter 14

That next day as she was finishing up her close-of-day routine, the last customer having left an hour ago, Ursula experienced her first storm on Harbourtown.

More than a little frightened by the way the windows rattled and the building seemed to tremble, she joined David and Tanya at the Inn, surprised to find more than a few people gathered there.

Vaguely, she wondered if Pierre would be there too, but then she remembered that harbourmaster and lighthouse keeper duties during a storm kept a man at work.

Her mind turned to Oxander - Quentin's spare room overlooked the beach at Bountiful Bay, or so he had told them. That was where Oxander would spend at least two months of recuperation; he could only return home when he was able to walk. A pang of guilt stabbed at her.

Vimto remained the same friendly but independent cat, despite his so-called master's absence. She made sure that she made an extra fuss over him, buying pet supplies next time she visited the mainland: two cat dishes, one for food, one for water. On a whim, she had purchased a feather on a long plastic rod, wondering then if Vimto would know what to do with the toy. She would have to teach him…

Jumping out of her thoughts as the thunder growled above them, she saw lightning lit up the outside darkness. Going to the window, she was warned not to. Patrons of the Inn were amazed that she didn't know the rules and the dangers. Aware of the lesson she'd learned earlier when questioning Pierre on the lifeboats, she kept her knowledge to herself.

"Do you not know the lightning 30/30 rule, girl?"
Ursula shook her head.

The man who'd spoken first tutted. "If it's less than 30 seconds before the thunder rolls after a lightning flash, the lightning is near enough to pose a threat."

"A lot of people thought that being in a car is the safest place during a thunderstorm, but it isn't. If there are no buildings to shelter in, then a car is better than being out in the open." Another man piped up.

One person began, and several joined in with the same knowledge, weaving the same story.

"A lightning storm does not have to be close for lightning to strike - it can strike up to 15 miles away from a thunderstorm, even if it's not raining."

Ursula gasped at that one. Several people nodded. "It can hit water too?" She asked.

A chorus of disbelieving grunts could be heard.

"Now," David warned them, "none of you knew until you were told." He turned to Ursula. "Being in the water is the worst place to be in a storm. To be scientific, lightning happens when the negative charges (electrons) in the bottom of the cloud are attracted to the positive charges (protons) in the ground. A bolt of lightning heats the air along its path causing it to expand rapidly. Thunder is the sound caused by rapidly expanding air."

"Right." Ursula replied, but the explanation was lost on her. Not that she was going to admit it. "Why is it so dangerous to be in the water?"

"Lightning doesn't strike the ocean as much as land, but when it does, it spreads out over the water, which acts as a conductor. It can hit boats that are nearby, and electrocute fish that are near the surface."

She gasped again. "All the fish die?"

David shook his head, knowing that he'd have to speak in simpler terms. "No, only those on the surface. Usually they are deeper down, and are unaffected."

Ursula nodded. That made sense. "What happens first - thunder or lightning?"

"If you are watching the sky, you'll see the lightning before you can hear any thunder." Someone answered.

"Light travels through air much faster than sound." David agreed.

Ursula hesitated. She wanted to ask why you'd be watching the sky in the first place, but she decided it sounded like a stupid question, so she didn't voice it. "Are many people killed by lightning?"

"What's the latest figure?" David cast his gaze across the room.

"I read 24,000. That's deaths. Then there's those who are injured - the figures on injured persons are around ten times that." A voice replied.

"Good God!" Ursula's eyes bugged out. It was a short while before she spoke again. "So, that rule is for water outside." It was more of a suggestion than a question.

David shook his head. "Lightning can strike exterior electric and phone lines, so you should unplug anything you have charging and not use power tools, computers in fact any appliance, even the shower. Especially as lightning can travel through plumbing."

"I thought that was an old wives' tale." Ursula managed.

Everyone was shaking their heads in disagreement.

"Stay away from windows and doors, and definitely don't sit on an open porch to watch a thunderstorm. Interior rooms are safest." One man stated.

Ursula's eyes searched around the room nervously. "This isn't an interior room, it has windows." A tremor was in her voice.

"We'll be fine as long as there's nobody at the windows or

doors." David reassured her.

"And nobody uses their phone." Ursula added.

He shook his head. "As long as they are not charging, there's no danger using a mobile phone."

"I didn't know that." Ursula was more and more astounded. "What else should I know?" She looked around. "How long after it goes away can we start doing things again - an hour?"

"Half an hour is fine." Several people spoke at once.

"You can tell when the storm is moving off by counting the seconds between thunder claps. It takes five seconds per mile."

"Seven," someone argued.

"No, five. Approximately five." The original speaker argued back.

Everyone looked at David for confirmation. "Five." He nodded.

This started off various conversations amongst the patrons.

Chapter 15

As everyone around them talked, she noticed Nolan sitting alone in the corner. He too was listening intently, giving her a smile when their eyes met. Bringing her drink over to him, she forgot all about her fears as she sat down beside him.

"I'm surprised Roger isn't here too." She began.

"So am I," Nolan frowned thinking about his absent partner. "He said he was going to make some repairs before going home, so maybe he finished up early when he saw the storm coming." He shrugged.

"Speaking of early, don't you have to get up very early each morning?"

Nolan pulled a face. "Yes, while everyone else is still tucked up in their warm beds." He laughed at himself. "But I knew the sacrifice when I became a fisherman."

"What about tomorrow?"

"What about it?" he teased her. "I'll just have less sleep tonight and catch up the next night." He shrugged. "It happens. You could say it's an occupational hazard."

Keen to impart some of her newly learned knowledge, Ursula nodded. "Not as dangerous as being in the RNLI."

Nolan gave her a funny look. "We are all RNLI crew here."

"Really?" She gasped.

"Really," he suppressed his laughter. "I'm shocked you didn't know. Yves and Oxander took me out for my first run over the territory the other night, when Oxander had his... misfortune."

"Don't." Ursula groaned. "I feel terrible. I had no idea what trouble I made for him, poor Oxander."

"You weren't to know," Nolan consoled her, draining his glass, "you're a townie."

Ursula was more surprised by the way she reacted to his

calling her a townie than his actual words. She didn't want to be a townie, she wanted to fit in here.

"Like you say, I need to get to bed." He stood up.

"But you can't go out in that!" Her expression was horrified.

"It's easing off. It'll have blown over in a few minutes. Can't you hear the wind has dropped?"

Lost for words, she shook her head.

Nolan smiled at her. "Of course not, you're a townie, look who I'm talking to. Goodnight Ursula."

With that, he was gone.

Last night's storm had cleared the air, delivering a beautiful late May morning with sunshine and singing birds everywhere. That was a great sign for today's birder tours, Ursula knew. Hopefully it also meant they'd be keen to part with their money in order to get a worthy souvenir of the day.

Ursula looked up as Walter arrived at the shop and sat down without saying anything, shaking his head. Tanya arrived from the adjoining door, heading straight to him, much to Ursula's puzzlement. Looking across into the café, she saw Eddie and Alicia were also clueless, and knew that she wasn't alone in not knowing what was going on.

"Terrible," Walter mumbled, still shaking his head.

"A terrible way to die." Tanya agreed.

Ursula's eyes widened, she drew closer; she saw Eddie and Alicia move nearer also.

"Who died?" Eddie asked, putting his arm protectively around Alicia as he spoke.

"Roger was found in his boat this morning, heart attack. He'd been out, all night, in that storm." Walter spoke haltingly. "We couldn't do anything." His voice cracked.

The younger trio gasped.

Tanya hugged him then. "Nobody could have done

anything." She shook her head sorrowfully.

"Hopefully that meant he didn't suffer." Alicia offered.

Ursula nodded her agreement, unable to find her voice. She had never known anyone who had died, even at 23, all of her family were still living. Unfortunately, she added to that thought.

"Does he have family? In Conning?" Eddie asked.

"Nobody. Last member of the Shoal family." Walter's voice was soft. "The best fishermen we ever knew in the area, the Shoals. Born to their work."

Ursula couldn't help thinking that with a name like Shoal that Walter was right. She thought then of Alicia, and smiled at her. "Like you, you were born to run a café or tearoom with such a name as yours."

She received sad smiles in reply.

"He told me, once, that he wanted a burial at sea, when the time came." Walter smiled faintly with his thoughts. "Seawater was in his veins, old Roger. God bless him."

Tanya nodded. "That sounds like him." Looking up, she saw David standing in the doorway.

"We'll hold the wake here." He announced.

"That'll be a long time yet." Ursula frowned. "Don't they have to do post mortem and funeral stuff first?"

Everyone shrugged.

"Quentin has already signed the death certificate." Walter told them. "I'll let you know when I do." He seemed to pull himself together a bit. "I should be off."

David came into the shop properly then, a glass of amber coloured liquid in his hand. "Drink this before you go. It must have been a terrible experience for you."

"True that." Walter nodded, thanking him. "Terrible." He repeated.

Chapter 16

Shona was working an extra evening shift at The Empty Tankard when the rumour reached her that Roger's death was not an accident. He was killed by Nolan because his training was overly stretched out; he wasn't receiving his proper share of the profits and he snapped, wanting what was rightfully his.

Having heard from Tanya and David how polite and hard working Nolan was, she doubted it very much. Besides, Quentin had ruled the death from a heart attack, likely due to natural causes, although nobody could fathom why Roger had been out in his boat during a storm. He of all people knew the risks.

It seemed Shona wasn't the only one to doubt that rumour.

"Do you not remember seeing what happens when lightning hits water?" The speaker was Will, one of the three lifeguards from Bountiful Bay beach.

"Yeah, why do you think we tell people to get out of the water?" Added in Dwayde, another of the lifeguards. "We ain't doing it to spoil your fun."

Marrisa was the third lifeguard, she shook her head. "It must have been a terrible sight when they found him. Poor Nolan must be so upset." She looked around them. "As for anyone thinking he could possibly have killed Roger." She snorted. "Roger treated him more like a son than a co-worker."

Muttered conversations flew up all over the place, and behind the bar Shona offered them a smile of thanks. She offered them a top up of their drinks, knowing Isaac wouldn't mind - after all, the lifeguards didn't drink alcoholic beverages.

Suddenly Isaac was behind her - he put down a plate of

fresh warm garlic bread, a known favourite of the lifeguard trio. Flashing a smile at Shona, who looked a bit guilty until then, he told them it was 'on the house' and wished them a good evening. Before returning to the kitchen, he asked Shona if she wanted to check up on Ursula.

"Why?" Shona frowned.

"It sounds like the island is in mourning." He explained. "Dad has arranged for the wake to be held at the Inn. I did offer to have everyone here, but he thought it was more poignant to use the Inn."

"I can see why he thought that. Although if it's a big turnout it would make better sense to be here." Shona drifted back to the bar, walking with him. "Let's see what happens." She smiled at him. "When you next speak to him," she began as Isaac was about to disappear.

"Yes?"

"Ask him about Nolan." Shona nodded at the table where the lifeguards were. "Marissa is right, it would have come as a terrible shock to him."

Isaac smiled and nodded. And for a moment there, he'd thought Shona was going to say her step-sister's name! Was there no love lost between the two?

At the Inn back at Harbourtown, Ursula remembered the conversation from the previous night about what happens when lightning hits water. She tried to console Nolan, who was sitting in the corner with tears in his eyes, an untouched drink in front of him.

An argument around them as to the true list of do's and don'ts in a storm made Ursula realise why Tanya had suggested that she talk to Nolan. They were about the same age and both, to a small degree with Nolan, were outsiders.

"Come on, let's get you home. It won't do any good sitting

amongst this rabble." Ursula stated, pulling at Nolan's arm as if to hurry him to his feet.

He stared at her uncomprehendingly.

"It'll be much more peaceful and easier to talk." She elaborated. "Is it far?"

Nolan swallowed hard. "Not far," he managed.

"Good." Ursula smiled. "Lead the way."

His expression was one that was as if a rabbit was caught in the headlights of an oncoming car. "N-no. I'm fine." He dashed off without her.

Ursula shrugged, returning to the bar stool at the end of the counter where she usually perched. As she was about to speak, she noticed Vimto's arrival, and smiled.

"Hello handsome Vimto." She greeted him. "Would you like a drink?"

On the other side of the bar, David raised his eyebrows. "I'm not giving that cat any more beer. He stayed all night the last time, burping and farting something chronic he was!"

Ursula and several of the other drinkers laughed. David had a shallow dish with water prepared, and set it down on the floor beside Vimto.

"No more jumping onto my counter, understood?" He shook a telling finger at Vimto.

Giving him a look, he gave a meow and bent his neck to drink the fresh water gratefully.

"It should be milk you give him." Ursula scolded.

"Cats can't tolerate our milk, there's special cat milk." A voice from the crowd stated.

"I didn't know that." Ursula blushed, looking down at Vimto she apologised. "What about the olives - were they okay for your stomach?" She asked him.

He looked at her for a while, let out a meow and jumped into her lap, nuzzling into her chin.

"Aww, you are the sweetest!" She made a fuss over him, as she knew he loved. "Come to the shop sometime, I've got a few things for you." She told him, wondering if he knew what she meant. Did cats know English or did they only speak Cat? She almost laughed with her thoughts. "Are you missing Oxander? Is Pierre being good to you?"

"I am, if he lets me." Pierre said, appearing at her elbow. "I was curious where this one was going and couldn't believe it when he came in here. Don't let the authorities catch him in the pub!"

"He comes in of his own accord." David shrugged. "Sniffs around, sits by the fire, charms a few guests and leaves when he wants."

"You know cats. They go wherever and whenever they want." Pierre replied, allowing Vimto to nuzzle into his pro-offered hand.

Inwardly he was relieved that Vimto received such a good reception, having followed him into the Inn, he half wondered if he was going to get the blame for the cat being out; half wondering how he was going to redeem himself over the error of letting the animal out of his sight.

Chapter 17

Oxander was the centre of attention on the hovercraft as people clustered around him to check on his welfare and lend their sympathy. He soon tired of the bombardment of questions, glad when Yves called a halt to the short trip out to sea - they had arrived at the precise place to give Roger's ashes the sea burial the fisherman had requested.

Walter had known Roger the longest, but he insisted on having Nolan beside him; he also coerced the young man to release the ashes with him, half each.

The trip back was made in a subdued silence.

Quentin took charge of the wheelchair he'd hired to help Oxander be a part of the event, driving his patient carefully along the cobbled quay side to the Inn so that they could join the commemoration group.

Ursula hadn't gone out with them, staying at the Inn to hold the fort, although without the ferryboat in operation there wasn't a flood of arrivals to Harbourtown that morning. To be fair, there were still a few tourists around. Alicia and Eddie too remained present at the café, so she wasn't alone; something she was glad for.

Even Caitlin had no duties that morning - no tour work and not even her regular gardening at the Treduggan family home up on the hill. She had been given the day off in the circumstances, and took this time to join the rest of the islanders.

Isaac had a pub full on the mainland, and they linked up with the Inn when the boat returned via an Internet connection on the large screen TV. In the end, there were so many people wanting to join the memorial, they did use both premises.

Only now did Ursula have the chance to speak to

Oxander and apologise. She had to wait for the right moment to get peace to speak with him.

"Oxander, I…"

"Don't." He began, cutting her off. "I don't want you anywhere near me."

"It was an accident," Ursula tried.

He glared at her. "How could you have been so stupid. Do you ever think?"

Again Ursula had the notion that she perhaps shouldn't speak. "I meant well," she went with.

Oxander scoffed.

"I really think she is telling you the truth." Yves interrupted.

"I really don't care." Oxander replied in much the same manner.

Ursula's face fell. "I've been looking after your cat for you." She gave it one more try.

"So has Pierre - and anyway he's not my cat, why does everyone think that he is?" Oxander snarled. "Leave me alone!"

"I'm only…"

"Get away from me!" He shouted.

Ursula scuttled away, almost in tears.

"Aren't you being a bit mean?" Caitlin challenged him.

"Mean?" A glint was in Oxander's eyes, and not one she liked the look of. "I could have been killed."

"No, you weren't."

"I wasn't, but I might have been. Thank God Quentin came to my rescue and convinced me I needed hospital treatment. I wanted to carry on if he would have helped me." His face changed. "They had to pin my leg bones together, and I narrowly avoided a blood clot on the brain."

The crowd around them gasped.

"Is that true?" Yves turned to Quentin, who nodded. "You

really could have died." His voice tailed off.

"I told you!" Oxander was furious. "I would have, if it hadn't been for Quentin." He gave the doctor a grateful smile.

"You'll heal." He nodded, playing down the importance of his role in the drama. "You were lucky," he admitted.

An hour later, he took Oxander back to Bountiful Bay. They left a slightly lighter atmosphere at the Inn, everyone telling stories about their best Roger memories. It had been too much for Nolan; he had disappeared after around twenty minutes.

Therefore, Ursula was most surprised to find Nolan appeared at her elbow no later than an hour later. He quietly apologised for running away from her the other night and rebuffing her friendliness; inviting her for coffee at his apartment.

Catching Tanya's eye across the room, she nodded and Ursula nodded back, telling Nolan that she was happy to accept his invitation and she was ready to go when he was. He smiled and linked arms with her, taking her up narrow street paths and winding steps until he stopped and took out his key.

They talked for a while, and he indeed did make her coffee. Drifting with his thoughts, Ursula put her hand on his arm to break him from his reverie - causing him to jump at her touch, the grip on his coffee slipping and the hot liquid spilling over his arms and across his lap.

Jumping up to run to the small kitchen, she quickly soaked a dishcloth and rushed back to him, dampening down his trousers and shirt sleeves.

"Shit! That hurts!" He exclaimed, moving past her to the kitchen to dowse his arms under the running tap.

"Stay there for at least ten minutes." Ursula advised. "You'll need to dress the burns properly."

Nolan shook his head. "Burns need to be left airing, dressings can allow infection to settle." He swore under his breath in pain.

"Oh Nolan, I'm so sorry! I didn't mean to make you jump!" Ursula bit her lower lip.

"It was an accident - you weren't to know I was a million miles away!" He gave her a small smile.

"Please get your arms properly checked out in a few days." She didn't return his smile, riddled with guilt. First Oxander, now Nolan - was she cursed or some kind of a jinx? "Promise me."

He nodded. "I will. I won't be able to untangle the nets otherwise." The thought struck him.

"You'll be in pain all the time, let me help you won't you. Anything you need, please let me know." Ursula felt overwhelmed now with guilt and horror.

"I will, but don't worry, please. It'll be fine." He tried to reassure her. "You're so sweet to be concerned." Leaning over, he kissed her cheek. "I want to ask you something, but I'm not sure this is the right time."

"Oh?" Ursula's interest was piqued. "Go on, you can ask me anything." She realised Nolan was coming over shy, and found it endearing.

"I want to take you out on my boat." He cleared his throat noisily. "A moonlit trip to Seal Point. What do you think?" He hesitated. "I mean, if you want to. If you trust me to look after you."

"Of course I do!" She gushed. "That sounds lovely." She beamed at him, kissing his cheek in return. "Please make sure your arms are okay first though." Her smile turned into a frown.

"It's a deal." He promised.

Chapter 18

Pierre sat down at one of the Inn's tables to tell Ursula about Cornish place names and what they meant, and about Cornish folklore. She had previously asked him to teach her things that she should know if she was ever going to cast off the 'townie' reputation. Falling for her charms, he agreed to help her.

The first groupings of names he'd made he explained were named after saints or parish saints. Some were relating to holy places or churches, some related to coves. That caught Ursula's attention, she skipped over the first list, finding that she recognised some of the names that were place names - Padstow, Launceston, Mevagissey. It was the information on coves that interested her more.

Par - Cove   Percuil - Narrow cove   Polperro - Cove + name Perro   Port Isaac - Cove + name Isaac   Porthallow - Cove of waterlillies   Porthleven - Cove of St Levan Portholland - Cove of the holy place   Porthpean - Little cove Porthtowan - Sand dune cove   Portloe - Sea lake cove Portreath - Cove in the beach   Portscatho - Cove of boats Praa Sands - Witch cove

Even she had to agree that some of the names made sense. Next there was a longer list awaiting her attention - these were translations.

Angarrack - The rock Bodmin - Dwelling of monks
Bolventor - Bold venture   Boscastle - Bottrel's castle
Cadgwith - Bushes   Camborne - Curve of the hill
Camelford - Curved river + ford
Carbis Bay - Cart bridge + bay

Cardinham - Hill fort   Carnkie - Dog carn

Carrick Roads - Rock anchorage

Chacewater - Stream in the hunting grounds

Delabole - Delyow stream   Devoran - Wet valley

Dobwalls - Two woods (French doublebois)

Duloe - Between 2 rivers (East / West Looe rivers)

Falmouth - Original name Aberfal - Mouth of the river Fal

Fowey - Beech trees Fraddon - Small stream

Gillan - Creek   Golant - Field in the valley

Goldsithney - Feast of sithney

Goonharvern - Ploughed downs

Goonhilly Downs - Hunting downs

Hayle - Estuary   Helston - Old court

Hessenford - Hag's ford

Indian Queens - Named after a pub, possibly in reference to Pocahontas

Lanner - Clearing   Liskeard - Court

Lizardtown - High court + town

Looe - Sea lake   Lostwithiel - Wooded land

Ludgvan - Ash heap   Marazion - Little market

Nancekuke - Valley of...   Nanpean - Little valley

Pendeen - Headland with fort

Penryn - End of the slope   Penzance - Holy head

Polgooth - Goose pool

Praze-an-Beeble - Meadow of the pipe

Redruth - Red ford (from when mining tinting the water red)

Roseland - Promontory / peninsula + land

Scorrier - Mining term Seaton - Twisting river

Temple - Refers to the Knights Templar who had a church here

Tintagel - Fort + name

Tywardreath - House on the beach

"That sounds great - Tywardreath." Ursula smiled at him. "I'd like a house on the beach."

He returned her smile. "Wouldn't we all?"

"So it isn't all pirates and smugglers?" Ursula teased him, having some of her drink while he laughed.

"To be fair," Pierre began, "Cornwall's coastline was perfect for smugglers back in the day. Most of it was uninhabited and with not many revenue men on patrol, it was easy for the smugglers to land tea, alcohol and tobacco."

Ursula frowned. "Alcohol and tobacco I understand, but tea?"

Pierre nodded. "At the time, remember we're going back to the 18th century, in Europe tea could be bought for a sixth of the price. French brandy was a fifth of the price."

"Wow!" Ursula gasped. "No wonder they smuggled it in! How long did smuggling go on for?"

"By around 1840, the smugglers had been beaten into submission. The revenue men discovered all of the usual tricks, and some were even spies amongst the fishermen."

"That was when they used coves to hide the stuff until the dangers were over?" Ursula asked, vaguely remembering something she'd read somewhere.

"Oh yes, any remote cove really. Passages and tunnels were dug out to avoid detection when it was picked up."

"That's so clever." Ursula remarked.

"Dangerous." Pierre shook his head. "The minimum penalty was deportation to somewhere like Australia, some were even hanged for the crime."

"Why so severe!" Ursula's expression was sorrowful. "It's not like they did anyone any harm."

"Only the rich, fat cats of the government." Pierre raised his eyebrows. "Mostly, you'd be fined and the goods taken from you. It all depended on the person who caught you and what you were caught with."

She nodded. "I'll bet there are some great stories."

Pierre smiled. "Oh, there are. You'll find hundreds, I'm sure."

Ursula returned his smile and changed the subject.

Later that evening when she was in her room, she looked up smuggling legends.

'Once landed, much of the contraband made its way up the country. On windswept Bodmin Moor, Jamaica Inn is the best known of all smuggling haunts because of the famous novel by Daphne Du Maurier.'

Ursula paused in her reading to select the copy of the book that Tanya had leant her from the shelf above her bed. Initially she hadn't been interested enough to read it, but now perhaps she might. She continued to read:

'When pepper was taxed heavily, it became a popular item for smugglers. Tiny Pepper Cove, north of Porthcothan, takes its name from the boatloads of spice that were landed there. It was an archetypical smugglers' cove: the narrow entrance from the sea is fringed with jagged rocks. However, once inside any vessel would be hidden by the high cliffs, thus any unloading could be done safely and leisurely.'

'The Blue Bell Inn, St Ives was once the haunt of Dutch smuggler Hans Breton. It was said that he was in league with the devil. He paid duty on only one keg of brandy: however, this never seemed to empty - lasting him 22 years.'

'At Ludgvan, two miles northeast of Penzance, the customs officers could not sell seized liquor in 1748, because of the vast quantity smuggled in. Smugglers were asking 3/3 a gallon for the illegally imported liquor: the reserve price on the seized goods was 5/6.'

She laughed at that. It served the customs men right! And before that, the Dutchman Hans, how clever of him to have a never emptying keg of brandy. Where there's a will, there's a way - she thought to herself.

'Cawsand and Kingsand. The vast natural harbour of Plymouth had a naval presence throughout the 18th and 19th centuries. The city itself formed the largest market for contraband in Cornwall, so it's not surprising to find some notorious villages nearby. Goods brought into the twin villages of Cawsand and Kingsand could be easily ferried across the harbour to Plymouth. Both towns were hotbeds of smuggling — in 1804 the revenue services estimated that 17,000 kegs of spirits had been landed here in just one year.'

'The open beaches of Whitsand Bay made a fine landing when the coast was sufficiently clear for covert runs, but smugglers seeking a more discreet approach brought goods ashore on Looe Island. In West Looe Ye Olde Jolly Sailor was a smuggler's haunt, and here too the story is told of how the quick-thinking landlady once concealed an illicit keg beneath her petticoats during an unexpected search. While the preventives searched, she calmly knitted.'

Hooting with laughter at what she'd read, Ursula suddenly realised the time was getting late. Far too late to start reading anyway. She went to sleep that night dreaming of cargo washing up on the shore from wrecked pirate boats.

Chapter 19

Vimto sauntered in as usual, tail held high as he pranced into the middle of the room. Sitting down at his now usual place by the fireside, he looked around.

The last time he'd sat here, Caitlin had a group with her who had wanted to get up close and personal with him. Vimto hadn't shared the emotion, and had simply walked away without causing a scene.

He could have done quite easily - either by meowling or hissing at them until they withdrew, or by curling up and going to sleep, completely ignoring them. But they were strangers, he had no idea how they would react, so he didn't try either tactic.

"You do have the most gorgeous eyes!" Ursula told him when she saw he was there and made her way over to him, crouching down on the floor beside him and offering out her nearest hand.

He sniffed her and gave her hand a lick before taking a few steps closer to her.

"I've never seen a cat with such mixed markings." Tanya commented from behind the bar. "No wonder the kids call him Vimto."

Reassured that he knew she was a friend not a foe, he allowed her to stroke him.

Ursula chuckled delightedly when he nuzzled into her at the mention of his name. "Beautiful boy." She told him. "So very beautiful." Carefully she kissed his head; immediately he reacted, giving her a head boop as a loving gesture from one creature to another.

"Oh Vimto, you sweetie!" She exclaimed.

Tanya smiled. "He's got you under his paw." She teased.

"Dogs have owners, cats have staff." David agreed, seeing

Ursula and Vimto on the floor enjoying each other's company. "Remember that Ursula, when he wakes you at some Godforsaken time in the morning for food." Laughing, he left them to it.

"Oh!" Ursula's face lit up. "I'd love to have him sleep with me each night. Imagine how lovely it would be!"

"Whenever we had a cat in the bed, he took up all the room and left us squashed in the corner against the wall." Nolan said as he entered the Inn. He too crouched down beside Vimto and began to stroke him, sharing a smile with Ursula.

"I wouldn't mind that." She replied.

"You would in winter when the room is freezing cold and the wall feels like ice against your bare skin." Nolan joked.

They both laughed then.

He got to his feet then, stretching his cramped legs. "Would you like a drink?" He asked.

"Meow." Replied Vimto.

Nolan fake tutted. "I wasn't asking you."

Vimto gave him a wounded look, and Nolan laughed, reaching down to pat his head.

"Oh, alright then. I'll see what Tanya has for you." Merriment dancing in his eyes, he winked at Tanya, who reached under the counter for provisions.

"Since you insist on blessing the establishment with your presence Sir, I took the liberty of doing some shopping. I hope this is to your satisfaction." Glancing at the packet, she smiled. "Chicken and turkey; that sounds better than what I had for dinner!"

Vimto ran over to where she'd placed a saucer on the floor, licking his lips. She took out another saucer and this one contained a small amount of milk, cat milk she assured them. Deftly opening the resealable packet, she forked out half of it before resealing it. Seeing the scathing look he was giving her, she promised him the rest when he'd eaten the first lot.

Vimto didn't move, locking eyes with her.

"Oh, alright then." Tanya caved in, and reopened the packet, forking out the rest of the food. "Don't make yourself sick." She warned him.

"Eurgh." Nolan shuddered. "Nothing like the noise of a cat puking to get you out of bed in the morning."

"Nolan!" Ursula beseeched him.

"What?" He turned his twinkling eyes to her. "It's true. Tell her, Tanya."

"Oh, it's true alright." Tanya nodded. "Still want a cat?" She asked her.

"Definitely!" Ursula beamed. "So what if there's a few little accidents, the good things will outweigh the bad." She watched Vimto as he ate and lapped up the milk. They all paused, and true to form, Vimto belched.

"Manners!" Tanya scolded.

Vimto looked up at her with big round pleading eyes and meowed mournfully.

"That's okay, you're forgiven." She told him, stooping to pat his head.

When she disappeared into the kitchen with the newly empty saucers, Vimto made his way over to Nolan and nudged him until he showed him both of his palms. Delightedly, he began to lick.

Ursula frowned. "What is he up to?"

"It's the fish, I'm sure of it." Nolan took his gaze from the cat to her, and back again. "No matter how much I wash my hands, he still loves to lick them."

Ursula laughed gently. "Sounds like I'm not the only one who is under the paw, eh Vimto?"

Kim was viewing the horizon with his telescope as he usually did every morning at this time.

It was amazing to see the large cargo ships on the horizon moving swiftly and smoothly across the sea with their tremendously heavy loads. There was a string of them as this was part of the main shopping routine to and from Calais.

He much preferred to watch the smaller crafts - the pleasure boats and yachts, able to imagine himself skippering one of those. Pristine white bow cutting through the waves, making journeys in record timing. Inwardly he sighed. Until then, it was only a dream.

Not that he wasn't grateful for his adoption into the Treduggan family and the lifestyle he had been brought into, far from it. It was natural for him to want to know about his real family, as much as anything else. What was in his future? What was in his past that he didn't know of? There was so much uncertainty. Fists clenched in anguish, he tried to rearrange his thoughts. He needed to walk to clear his head.

In the garden, he found Caitlin on her knees digging furiously. Double checking the time, he frowned. Almost on cue, she looked up.

"It's okay, I have half an hour before the birders arrive for the morning tour." She gave him a warm smile. "How are you this morning?"

He returned her warm smile, but shrugged.

"My offer is always open." She reminded him. She had told him that whenever he wanted to join a tour, he could - free of charge.

He was grateful to her for the offer and for her kindness. "Maybe sometime. I'll take a walk and stop off in the village."

It still seemed strange to call the ex-barn area, where now the shop, café and Inn were, the village. But they all did it, so he too had adopted it.

"It does you good to have a walk in the fresh air." She nodded. "We are most fortunate to live here - imagine how stuffy and hot it must be in the city." She shuddered.

"Yuk," he agreed, also shuddering. "Rather them than me."

"Or me." Caitlin nodded. "Enjoy your walk. Maybe we'll see you at the Inn one night." She let the sentence hang in the air.

"Maybe. Thanks Caitlin. Have a good day." And with that, he was gone.

On a whim last week he'd stopped in the village and by chance, Eddie was on a break. They'd talked about the weather and business, and then football. Eddie's eyes had lit up when Kim confessed he was more into rugby, and the Penzance Pirates fans recognised each other.

He was rather looking forward to another conversation with Eddie, and had paid specific attention to the last Pirates match in preparation for their next meeting...

Chapter 20

Marissa, on shore and above the beach in the lifeguard hut, scanned their territory with her binoculars. She'd thought a moment ago that she had seen a boat drifting; refocusing, she saw that she had indeed been correct.

It was drifting in the stretch of water beyond Bountiful Bay, on the way out to sea. It was still too far out for her to make out the name, otherwise she could have put two and two together. It was an unusual sight, and a worrying one - on many levels.

"Guys," she called down to her two colleagues, pointing towards the horizon. "There's a boat out there, looks like it's drifting."

They both nodded. "We'll tether it."

Heading off purposely when they also spotted it, they knew it was safe to leave her alone on patrol for the short time it would take to get out to the boat and back again. Not many surfers or swimmers were out at the moment, and the usual rush of beachgoers hadn't yet arrived.

With Will steering, their rescue boat soon ate up the distance between them and the drifting vessel.

Dwayde exclaimed, recognising the boat now they were nearer. "It's The Storm, that's Nolan's boat. Where is he?"

Will frowned. "He should be heading back by now. I hope he's alright."

Once they were a few feet from The Storm, they saw that it wasn't unmanned - Nolan was slumped unconscious at the bottom of the boat. Both of them calling out as they pulled alongside and tethered their boat to his, Nolan began to come around.

"Marissa, call Quentin down, we have a casualty. We'll take him and the boat in." Will radioed, as Dwayde jumped across from their boat to Nolan's.

"No, don't get up yet." Dwayde took him by the shoulders, stopping Nolan from sitting up. "Let yourself recover first. What happened?"

Will dropped their anchor to stop both boats drifting further, before he too jumped across.

"I..." He faltered. "I don't know." Nolan closed his eyes again.

"Did you feel okay when you left this morning?" Will asked him, trying to jog his memory.

"I guess so."

"How do you feel now?" Dwayde had his fingers on Nolan's wrist, monitoring his pulse.

"I'm not really sure." Nolan confessed.

"You need to be checked out. By the time we get you back, Quentin will be waiting for us." Dwayde looked around for Will, seeing he was at the end of the boat where the nets were in the water.

He returned to them in a few strides. "You cast the nets but they aren't open." His frown deepened.

"Did I?" Nolan opened his eyes. "I don't remember."

They could both see he was becoming upset.

"That's alright, don't worry about it. No harm done." Will patted him on the shoulder lightly. "I'll have them wound up again and we'll take you to Quentin, you and the boat." He looked at Dwayde.

"Tell me when you're ready, I'll take us to shore. It's probably best if one of us stays here." He pulled a face.

"Good idea." Will nodded. "Give me a minute." In several strides he was at the mechanism and a whirring began.

Nolan groaned and clutched at his head, screwing his eyes closed at the noise. It was as if it was splitting his head in two.

"Won't be long." Dwayde consoled him. "You feel very hot." He frowned. "Are you running a fever?"

Even the gentle lapping of the waves against the boat was making Nolan feel sick. He wasn't able to answer; passing out again.

At the beach landing area, Quentin and Marissa awaited the boats. Nolan was able to get out of the boat by himself, although Will had his arm around him protectively. Legs shaking, he almost collapsed into the awaiting support chair.

"We've got you Nolan, it's okay." Dwayde soothed him.

"High temperature, queasiness and fainting fits." Will relayed to them.

"It sounds like an infection," Quentin frowned, relieved to not have another dead fisherman on his hands. "What have you been up to, young man?"

Nolan groaned in reply.

"Let's get you lying down." Pulling up the shade on the chair, Will too was aware that he was glad Nolan was alive, even if he wasn't well.

"I'll call over to Harbourtown, someone will be looking for him soon." Marrisa stated as they took Nolan up the pier and across the beach.

Under the lifeguard hut was the first aid station, a bench earmarked for lying a casualty down. She knew that was where they'd initially take him, before deciding what next step was necessary. Radioing across to Pierre, she relayed the facts and promised an update when they had one.

"I'll leave you with Will and Quentin. You're in good hands." She heard Dwayde say when she got back.

Smiling at her colleague when he appeared beside her in the hut, she nodded at him. "How is he?"

"Much improved. Well spotted." He clapped her on the

shoulder. "The current had hold of the boat, we had to anchor before we could both get to him."

She took his praise in her stride. "Well done." She praised him in return. "I hope he'll be okay. I'm starting to wonder if there's a jinx on Harbourtown."

"A jinx?" Dwayde laughed, glad to have a lighthearted moment. "No, it's just life." He shrugged. "Things happen."

"I suppose." But she wasn't so sure.

Chapter 21

Ursula was daydreaming about the moonlight ride in Nolan's boat, sea spray in the air, wind in her hair. It was beautiful how the moonlight was reflected in the calm water; she'd been pleasantly surprised that not everything was pitch black, more shades of black, deep blue and greys.

Nolan's pale, freckled face bathed in moonlight looked fantastic, especially when he kissed her.

"Ursula!" Alicia nudged her hard.

"Ow!" She exclaimed, holding her side. "What was that for?"

"You're in another world, and there are customers." Alicia left her to it then, glad that Ursula soon returned to her normal charm offensive.

"She is a real blonde." Eddie chuckled.

Alicia gave him a look. "I'm a blonde, so what are you insinuating?" She teasingly whipped at him with the tea towel, sending him scuttling back into the kitchen.

"What?!" Caitlin, Ursula, Tanya and Eddie gasped at the same time.

David had been alerted earlier by Pierre, and had called Isaac on the mainland to appraise him of the situation, before then calling up to the Treduggan house with the news.

Yves was out in the midst of conveying passengers to Conning before collecting a new group for the return to Harbourtown. Alicia had nipped across on an earlier journey with Yves and was due to arrive back with him on this trip.

"Quentin says he'll be fine at home and after a few days rest, be back to normal." David told them. "Walter will keep an eye on him during his rounds."

Ursula began to cry, glad of Tanya's arms around her then.

"Thank God someone saw him." Caitlin spoke then.

David nodded. "Marissa spotted the boat with her binoculars. It was drifting out to sea off Bountiful Bay."

Ursula cried harder at this. Everyone knew of their special moonlit boat trip - in such a small place, nothing was a secret.

"You should see him later, put your mind at rest." David suggested to her.

"Yes," Tanya nodded at her husband, "that's a good idea. I'll come with you." She gave Ursula a squeeze. "Come on, come and sit down and I'll make you a tea."

"No," Ursula shook her head, sniffing. "No, thank you Tanya, I can't. I have the shop to look after."

"It's okay," Eddie found his voice. "I can run both for a while. Alicia will be back soon too."

"Oh Eddie!" Ursula threw herself into his arms. "Thank you so much!"

"Or later, when you want to see him. Just say."

"You're so wonderful!" Ursula grinned, kissing his cheek.

"What the hell is going on!" Alicia roared, seeing Ursula kissing her partner and him blushing furiously.

"I'm only thanking him, no need to get all jealous." Ursula pouted.

Fuming, Alicia pulled Eddie away from the group, the kitchen door slamming shut behind them.

"Uh oh, I sense a domestic." David teased.

Eddie watched the steam pouring from Alicia's ears. He allowed her to rant, knowing that the café was currently empty; any drifting customers would be attended to by either Ursula or Tanya.

"It is true, she was only thanking me. She is nothing to me other than a friend, as she is with you." He took Alicia's hands, wondering if this was the right time...

"I'm not sure if I should believe you." Alicia saw his expression change. "I trust you, Eddie. It's her I don't trust, she goes after every man she sees."

Eddie wanted to laugh but from her expression, he decided not to. "I'm glad that you trust me. I promise you, nothing would happen between me and Ursula. You are the one I love. You only." Squeezing her hands, he waited until she looked up. "In fact, I think it's time I showed you how much you mean to me." Grinning at her, he let go of her hands, and got onto one knee. "Alicia, you are my partner and my soul mate. I never want to be with anyone but you. Will you marry me?"

Totally thrown off guard, Alicia's hands flew up to her mouth as she gasped.

"You'd make me the happiest man on Earth if you said yes." He continued. With one hand, he took her left hand; with the other, he flicked open the ring box.

The summer sun shone brightly through the windows at that exact moment allowing the diamonds to glisten and sparkle.

"Eddie! That must have cost you a fortune!"

"You are worth it." He kissed her hand. "What do you say?"

She grinned at him. "Yes. Yes, I will take you to be my lawfully wedded husband." She teased, laughing when he did; watching as he carefully took the ring from the box and slid it onto her finger and perfectly over the knuckle. "How did you get the right size?" She marvelled.

"Fate." He shrugged. "Like finding you, it was meant to be." Grinning happily, they embraced.

"I do love you, Eddie." She said in his ear.

"I'm glad of that, because I love you so very much." He whispered back.

Chapter 22

Nolan was asleep on the sofa when Tanya and Ursula came to visit that afternoon.

"We shouldn't disturb him." Tanya whispered.

"It's okay, I'm awake." Nolan replied, opening his eyes. "I take it Walter let you in."

They both nodded.

"How are you feeling, you poor soul?" Tanya bent over to hug him.

"Much better, thank you."

"Oh Nolan, thank God!" Ursula took Tanya's place, hugging him tightly. "We could have lost you and nobody would have known until it was too late. Why didn't you tell someone you weren't well?" She scolded him, pulling away from him.

"I can look after myself." He frowned.

"I agree with Ursula." Tanya shook her head. "You were lucky Marissa caught sight of the boat before it was too late."

"Don't over-exaggerate." He tutted, rolling his eyes.

Ursula was pursing her lips in disapproval, Tanya saw. She broke the news to him gently, thinking it was better to come from her rather than Ursula.

"You might not be aware of it, but when Will and Dwayde got to you, you were caught in a current and being pulled seaward."

His eyes widened.

"What caused the infection?" She asked, mindful of changing the subject before he had nightmares over it.

"These," he very carefully rolled up his sleeves to show them his newly dressed painfully burnt arms.

They both gasped.

"From the other night?" Ursula was horrified.

Tanya looked between the pair of them. Nolan nodded, explaining about the hot coffee he'd tipped over himself while he'd been talking with Ursula after Roger's wake.

Tanya winced, and seeing the look on Ursula's face, offered to make him a drink in order to give them time alone.

"Tell her, Tanya." He whined when she returned to the room. Ursula was standing over him, hands on hips, in full lecture mode. She could guess what she had been saying to him, and took pity on Nolan.

"He will be fine after a rest." She began, seeing the relief in Nolan's expression when she took Ursula a few paces away. "You heard what Quentin said."

"But someone should be here to look after him." Ursula argued back.

Glancing at him, she saw him frantically shaking his head: Tanya silently agreed. "It's not necessary, besides, as close as you two are, it isn't right to force yourself on him, poor Nolan. He's had a shock and he knows that we're here to support him, don't you?"

Nolan nodded. "I'm grateful, really I am." He smiled at them both. "I don't need to be watched, I'm much better than I was."

Ursula was torn between her conflicting reactions. "You are right." She sighed. "I'm sorry Nolan, I didn't mean to lecture you. I care about you."

Tanya nodded. "We all do." She hugged Ursula. "You gave us the fright of our lives when we heard what had happened." She turned to Nolan.

"I'll bet. I'm sorry." He hung his head.

"Do as Quentin says and you'll be right as rain soon." Tanya got him to smile.

"I hate that saying, it doesn't make sense." He complained, but he was smiling.

"We should go." She squeezed Ursula before letting go of her. "As long as you promise you'll call us if you want us."

"Of course." He nodded. "Thank you, honestly I had no idea. I owe my life to Will and Dwayde."

"And Marissa." Tanya pointed out.

Nolan nodded. "Yes, and Quentin. I must thank all of them."

"Plenty of time for that yet." Tanya smiled at him. "Make sure you eat properly, and keep your fluids up."

"Now you sound like Quentin." He teased. "I will." He nodded. "I'll be at the Inn when I feel up to it."

"Good." Tanya and Ursula both spoke together.

"Only when you feel up to it." Tanya warned him, hugging him goodbye. She hesitated.

"Can I catch you up?" Ursula asked her.

"Sure," she nodded, "but don't be too long, Nolan needs to rest." She saw Nolan's face flickered from fear to relief, letting herself out quietly when she heard the two youngsters begin to talk.

Shona had to admit that the shop was quieter without Ursula, but she was pleased and relieved to see that trade didn't drop off. In fact, those on Conning mainland were enjoying an increased revenue thanks to the new activities at Harbourtown. All of the promotional work and introductory discounts had worked a treat!

Speaking of treats, everywhere he went Vimto had something to enjoy - a drink here, some nibbles there. It wasn't only Ursula who spoiled him - even Pierre, a sworn dog lover, was paying special attention to his furry comrade.

There had been some rare bird sightings during several birder tours, and this generated excitement amongst the bird loving community, so much so that they reworked the schedule enabling Yves to take out a boatfull whilst Caitlin entertained guests on Harbourtown in the gardens and amongst the wildlife on the hill. After a bite in the café, the pair swapped over guests - doubling their revenue each day of the summer season in this way.

With a little bit of homework, Caitlin had taught Yves her part on dry land, so he was able to fulfil hosting roles both on and off Harbourtown. Their special project was proving more lucrative than they could have dared imagine!

Yves stopped off one evening with Caitlin at Roundhouse to see the Anchorage cousins, pleased to find that they too were having a successful season of bookings for vacations and day lessons.

He had the thought that they should really send a thank you to the Treduggan family, after all, it had been their idea to develop Harbourtown. Such opportunities they had all taken advantage of wouldn't have flourished without their vital input. However, he had no idea quite what they could do, and hit on the idea to involve Kim next time they saw him.

Chapter 23

Oxander requested that Quentin pick up Ursula on his return to Bountiful Bay so that they could talk. He had called to ask her to forgive him for his out of character shortness with her and apologise for the way he spoke to her so rudely.

Ursula was thrilled, and told him that any night after hours would be fine, whatever suited him and Quentin best - and did he need her to bring anything? He thanked her, refusing the offer and said he'd see her soon before disconnecting the call.

It seemed she had some kind of spell around her, as Kim had been dropping into the café and shop much more regularly in the past week, giving her smiles from a distance before coming over to enquire how business was doing and how she was getting on.

Walter was still a regular visitor, and she could have sworn he was deflecting attention to her. It was so liberating to have more than one man interested in her! Quentin was the only single man around who wasn't aware of her charms, would something happen on the way to see Oxander if she flirted also with him? The thought filled her with glee.

Yves explained about RNLI training and the difference between the lifeboats the next night they were all together at the Inn. Ursula was interested but also Nolan was learning, as this was different to what he'd come across on his training on the mainland.

"There are over 400 lifeboats?" Ursula gasped, sure that she had misheard.

Noland and Yves both nodded. "We patrol over 19,000 miles of coastline and inland waters, like the River Thames up in

London." Yves informed her.

"That's why there are two different categories of lifeboat - all-weather and inshore." Nolan added.

Ursula frowned. "All weather? Surely every lifeboat should be all weather?" She looked between Nolan and Yves.

"I don't think that's a suitable name really, of course all boats are all weather. Usually they are called upon when the weather is at its worst." Yves began. "Those called all-weather lifeboats can achieve high speed safely in any weather condition, they are self-righting also."

"It depends on where the lifeboat is in relation to other lifeboat stations as to which lifeboat is where." Nolan added. "We don't have a lifeboat station here, so we only have the inshore lifeboat."

"And the hovercraft," Yves put in. "It's different to the ferry hovercraft in that it is lighter, faster and stronger, and smaller."

"Do we need both?" Ursula asked.

"Inshore lifeboats are for closer to shore, shallow water, or near caves and rocky water. The hovercraft is for use when dealing with mudflats and river estuaries." Yves explained. "With the mud flats around Conning, Roundhouse and Harbourtown the hovercraft was deemed to be necessary."

Ursula nodded. "I read up about the Penlee disaster," she hesitated as their expressions fell. "How brave those men were, and the boat was only wooden!"

"We are much better equipped now, and with technology the improvements help us save more lives."

"How much does a lifeboat cost?" Ursula asked, pondering the question aloud.

Nolan also looked at Yves, he didn't know the answer to this.

"Our inshore lifeboat is an Atlantic 85," he nodded at Nolan, "an upgrade on the 75 you're used to. They are £214,000.

The hovercraft is around £400,000 - but the most expensive is the all-weather lifeboat. It is more than four times that price."

Nolan and Ursula both gaped at him.

"In any given year, it can cost from £163.5 million for the RNLI to run." Yves continued. "One crew member's training is nearly £1600."

Ursula tuned out of the technical specifications the two men went through. She knew enough. It was amazing, and so were the volunteers of the RNLI.

"The 85s are so much more advanced than the old 75s." Nolan agreed. "The engines, the 35 knots top speed, all of the updated rescue equipment."

"It's all the tech that impresses me. The self-righting, beaching without engine damage and inversion proofed engines that can be restarted after a capsizing." Yves shook his head with amazement. "Amazing."

Nolan agreed.

Isaac was polishing beer glasses at the counter of The Empty Tankard during a quieter spell, his mind across the stretch of water where his parents had been running Harbourtown Inn.

The time had simply flown by, and the tourists had really taken to the revamped village on Harbourtown island, but importantly, not forgetting Conning.

It was natural for Cecillia to be doubtful about the feasibility of the project, and as his wife, she had a right to air her thoughts on the future of their business. He was relieved in more than one way that her doubts had been unfounded.

His parents had been generous beyond his wildest dreams handing over The Empty Tankard to him. They had been more than happy to accept the challenge of building and sustaining a new business, even at a time when most people would be thinking of easing into retirement.

It had been an opportunity created by the Treduggan family that nobody on Conning had foreseen. Sure the café, and the shop to a lesser degree, were a brilliant boost of revenue for the village. He had to admit that he too was sceptical of the Inn's position; glad that he had kept his thoughts to himself. Not that if it had flopped it would have been the fault of either parent...

Chapter 24

Reading more and learning about the part of the country she now lived in and loved, Ursula decided to draw up a list of places she wanted to visit when she was able. She admitted that this would probably take place in the winter, when the tourist season had petered out and the place was much quieter, but that didn't really matter.

Cornwall was steeped in mining history, once the age of smuggling had its day. She didn't envy the workers, spending hours in dark, cramped conditions, but she could imagine the excitement when they came across a vein of tin, or iron, or whatever it was they were looking for.

Tourist attractions - but the little known ones and those that were more off the beaten track. Beaches and coves and the islands around them. There were also more than a few majestic large family homes and estates.

She wondered then if anyone had visited the Treduggan family home. They were a very quiet family, and Kim too was a quiet soul. Not much was known about them as a whole: it seemed that keeping themselves to themselves was how they preferred to live, and that was fine. Each to their own. They had given their agreement to have her run the Harbourtown shop and she was grateful.

Due to the frequency of the visits to Oxander over the last month, Quentin had grown somewhat used to Ursula. He did resent being used as a glorified taxi service, however. The fault was not hers, so he did not blame her.

Always he asked if she would prefer him to take her back to Harbourtown afterwards, but she always politely declined

- unless he had business out on one or other of the islands and therefore wasn't going out of his way. Sometimes he did, and that was fine; sometimes he didn't but he lied and said he did anyway.

He couldn't get away from the idea that he was responsible for her. It was a stupid thing to think, because he was quite sure that she would be most upset by the very thought.

To stave off the awkward silence between them, she asked about his work and his training - steering well clear of the subject of relationships. Gossip had told the story for him of his lost loves and Ursula was sure that it was impolite to pry when someone did not want to discuss the subject. Or be discussed.

Again she was struck by the fact that he and Shona would make a great pair; again, she kept the thought to herself as he informed her that his life would remain relationship free.

Every journey together, she made a point of telling him how wonderful he was to surrender his home and his time to Oxander's recovery; and that she hoped Oxander was grateful. It was after all a huge sacrifice: Quentin was a very private man, everyone knew. He always nodded and thanked her, replying that he hoped so. But that was it - the discussion was closed at that point.

Over the weeks, he grew used to Ursula and was therefore able to engage in basic conversation. In fact, he realised he would miss their conversations, in a strange way. The last time they took the double journey as Oxander would return to Harbourtown the following day, Ursula told Quentin of Shona's disastrous relationship history. She confided in him that Shona deserved happiness, much as he himself did.

Quentin's face was a picture! But the seed was sown...

Waves lapping against the stern of the Kernow Star where Kim had chosen to sit, he relaxed as he listened to the call of the birds around him.

It was too early for the first tour of the day to be around, and thus he had the place to himself. It would be this way for a while yet, as he knew the routine of everyone on the island.

Yves was already hard at work, ferrying people and supplies between the islands; he'd seen Caitlin already pulling at the never ending weeds in the Treduggan garden as usual. In the village below, Eddie and Alicia were no doubt already in the kitchen; David and Tanya would be making breakfast before preparing for the day ahead and Ursula too would be getting up. He never had a lie in; it seemed a wasteful practice. Far better to have an early night than a lie in the next morning.

Over on Roundhouse and on the mainland, the locals would be starting their own morning routines. The September sun was shining down on them all, promising a warm day to come. It was beyond idyllic, Kim couldn't help thinking. Or it would be, if only he had the perfect woman to share it with.

Sighing, he dictated the verse into his phone via the speech recorder. He could work on the new piece of prose later. Now it was time to let the sounds of nature around him soothe his wandering mind. It had become a habit to anchor the boat here and let his thoughts drift... Screaming of gulls brought him back from his thoughts - but he wasn't worried, knowing that it signified Nolan bringing in his morning's catch.

Those gulls were trying their luck to steal their breakfast without doing any work themselves - no matter how often they tried and failed, they still returned the next day. In a way their perseverance should be admired; but on the other hand...?

Kim was reminded that he needed to discuss with Nolan about how he was fayreing after the death of Roger and with the increased workload. Did he need help and would a replacement for Roger be necessary? Kim frowned, aware that he hadn't had the thought before and wondering why not. It wasn't as if it was such a ludicrous idea. Vowing to broach the subject with Nolan today, he rethought his own schedule so that it could coincide with the return of the young fisherman from his duties later that morning.

When he could, he took the boat out and listened in to the tourist chatter - mostly during, after and before a tour. Birder tours run by Caitlin were fully booked at the 15 person capacity and this seemed a trend that was not about to be broken any time soon.

It was an exciting time for the residents of Harbourtown, and he had news of another exciting project. A film crew wanted to record on the picturesque quayside.

Chapter 25

Oxander's return after two months of recuperation timed perfectly with Nolan and Ursula's relationship cooling off. Kim's attention too had faded: she didn't see him as often as before. However, she received anonymous messages containing poetry and love notes every so often.

She had her suspicions who the sender was - someone who was a romantic at heart; despite the moonlit boat trip, that wasn't Nolan. He was practical and proper: he spoke as he found and he didn't mince his words.

Neither, she felt, were they from Quentin - the mysterious, brooding doctor. She had tried to break through his self preservation barricades, but nothing was giving. If she thought about it, she could see Shona and Quentin getting along well, but she didn't say anything. Not once had Shona been in touch since throwing her out. That was fine, Ursula had friends here now and she was happy, that was all that mattered.

Possibly, the special attention she was receiving came from Oxander. He may have been pining for her whilst in recuperation; after all, they had developed a relationship of sorts.

Nobody knew exactly what was going on in the lighthouse. The outside was being painted and repaired, and thus was surrounded by a network of scaffolding. All hours of the day and night men took boxes and cases, and tools, into the structure; hammering and banging echoed around the peacefulness of Harbourtown for several days.

On the fourth day, Oxander's sixth day of his return, he

supervised the removal of the scaffolding and signed off the work that had been done. He now had the smartest lighthouse in the area, he boasted.

However if anyone questioned what had been done, he vaguely answered "upgrades and maintenance" - to even the most non technical person, this sounded like a fobbing off sort of answer.

It had to be said that the team of men had done an excellent job - the lighthouse looked as if it was brand new. They had worked with remarkable speed and care, and once more, Harbourtown became peaceful.

Although it was a working harbour, the boats dropping off their cargoes were untroublesome. Their men always docked at the same points, unloaded carefully and filled in the necessary forms and paperwork without complaint. Oxander had no issues with them getting in the way of the pleasure crafts or the hovercraft Yves used to transfer people and supplies to and from Conning and the Islands.

On the other side of the harbour, the beach was submerged when the tide was in - and when it was out, beachgoers could allow their children to play in the clean sands and, if they so desired, swim in the shallower water safely. Out in Bountiful Bay, they had designated surf and water activities areas that were patrolled by the lifeguards, and nobody got the two areas confused.

This helped Oxander immensely to maintain a high safety standard within the confines of Harbourtown. On the other side of the island, by the swampy mudflats, the RNLI hovercraft was kept. Restrictions on the vessels meant that Yves couldn't use the Oceanmaster - his regular working hovercraft - on RNLI business; they had an inshore lifeboat, Towednack, stationed permanently at Harbourtown for most of the training and any emergency calls that were received.

Overall, the harbour had a calm atmosphere. The wooden baulks that offered the harbour protection during the most severe storms could be hoisted into position to barricade the harbour opening by machine within ten minutes. This offered vital protection, and allowed time to launch the lifeboat in case it was needed before the harbour was effectively shut off.

The plan to access Towednack when anchored off Harbourtown was to take the hovercraft out to it; this was why Nolan's training had to involve learning how to manoeuvre the unusual vessel. Usually, they would have taken a motorboat out, but this would make better sense.

The rescue team needed four people, but during the worst storms they would need a crew of at least five, preferably six, to keep everyone safe. If need be, Quentin's own motor boat could be tethered to the hovercraft until the lifeboat returned.

Logistics of such an operation were worked out between the rescue team, and with most of the villagers as volunteers there shouldn't ever be a long wait until they had enough people to launch an emergency rescue service.

Yves took in Nolan's look of horror. "Consider it just a funny looking boat." He suggested.
His teasing words had worked - Nolan laughed, his tension diluted.
"It is funny looking!" He teased back. "What sort of boat has a skirt?"
Yves laughed, and patted his back, watching him as Nolan was trying to take everything in.
"How does it actually work?" Nolan asked as he walked all around it.

"The cushioned parts are called sponsons, there are two of them. The twin engines provide lift and propulsion through the fans, and also electrical power for navigation, communication and searchlights. The lift created means the craft can fly over mud, sand and shallow water - two fans build up air pressure under the craft; the thrust is provided by two large fans on the back that act in the same way as aeroplane propellers."

"Cool!" Nolan exclaimed. "Some engines."

Yves smiled at him. "Two VW 1.9 turbo diesel engines." He elaborated.

"Must need a lot of fuel." Nolan frowned.

"They have a range of 3 hours at full speed and a fuel capacity of 127 litres, so it's much more economical than you'd think."

Nolan was very impressed.

"Before rescue hovercraft were introduced the only method of rapid access to areas like mudflats and quicksand was by helicopter. Surface access was limited to walking, using mud mats and crawling boards." Yves patted one of the sponsons. "Not only can they deflate for travelling by road - they have to by law anyway - these are great for keeping a large stable platform and offer a soft edge for casualty rescue. There is special mud rescue equipment onboard as well as the regular medical equipment."

"I was wondering about that." Nolan nodded. "How do you steer the thing?"

"These rudders," Yves moved down the craft to the back of it. "I'll show you."

Yves took him through the basics before they went anywhere - start up, steering, braking - only then did they manoeuvre off the mudflats. He made sure to tell Nolan to be careful where he docked the vessel as there was an extensive project ongoing on this part of the island. He didn't have to give any more information, Nolan had heard enough and could be trusted to be careful.

Switching over when they were on the water properly, Nolan gently accelerated and began to turn the craft as Yves directed. They went up and down the coastline; against the tide; across the waves; up to the beach at Conning and across the shallow water, mindful of the rocks.

His face creased with concentration, Nolan found that Yves had been correct - the hovercraft wasn't as cumbersome as it looked. He was relieved to be back on dry land, however he was beginning to admire the craft by the time their lesson was over.

"Next time I'll let you do it all and I won't say anything." Yves told him: Nolan's face was a picture.

They both laughed.

Chapter 26

Caitlin first heard the woodpecker in the trees by the gardens up at the Treduggan family home. Excitement flowing through her veins, she abandoned her trowel and kneeler pad where she'd been working at the weeds in the flowerbed and attempted to follow the noise.

"He's in there." Kim said from behind her, not wanting to make her jump. He pointed to a group of tall trees. "I built several nest boxes over the last few years." He confessed.

Caitlin's jaw fell open. "You did? Do they all get used?" Her cheeks were flushed warm.

"I have to say I'm not entirely sure." He smiled. "Part of me wanted to put cameras in, but part of me wanted them to have their privacy."

He grew in Caitlin's estimation with that one statement. She nodded eagerly. "I thought I detected a bit of a twitcher in you." She teased.

He actually laughed. "I love nature," he spread his hands wide, "what more can I say?"

Her ready smile was one that warmed him. "You could take your own tours." She half suggested, half offered.

"I'll leave that to the professionals." He smiled back at her. "Now, I'm not very sure as I saw it only once, but I thought I saw a treecreeper not far from here."

Caitlin's eyes widened. "That's a rare bird in this part of the world."

Nodding, Kim laughed. "I know. That's why I wasn't sure." The look on her face told him that she would find the answer to his question, one way or another. He plunged in with another of his ideas. "At the other side of the island, in the mudflats, I'd often wondered if it was possible to make something of them. Some sort of reserve."

Caitlin's eyes were saucer wide. "That's an excellent idea!" He inclined his head as if to say that he thought so too.

"We really need to get together to talk all this through properly." Sensing the moment, she jumped on it before it was gone again. "But not now, obviously. You're busy I'm sure, and I have another touring day fully booked."

"Another time, Caitlin."

"Definitely, yes!" She grinned at him, getting an urge to hug him, but she quashed it not wanting to scare him off.

He bade her farewell and disappeared.

They did indeed have a somewhat large array of birds that weren't British, that had been blown off course on their way to and from other lands. Caitlin's personal favourite had to be the sunny plumage of the American Golden Oriole. Its song too was a treat. At times like this, she felt very privileged to live in this wondrous place.

As if to encourage her further, the woodpecker began again to drum and drill.

"Can I come in?" Quentin's gaze fixed on the back room of the shop.

Shona was flummoxed, firstly by the uninvited guest and now by his intention to stay beyond a quick chat. Overall, she had seen Quentin maybe a handful of times - they knew who each other was, but that was about all.

"I thought I picked a quiet time to talk to you, but I won't take you away from your work." He reassured her. "I don't mind if you have to desert me." He teased.

Shona was now even more confused. Her expression belied her thoughts.

He decided to plunge in. "I've been talking to your sister."

"Step-sister," she interrupted.

"Oh. Sorry." Quentin paused. "I didn't mean to cause offence." He apologised.

"No, no problem." She gave him a forgiving smile. "Is everything okay?" Her smile gave way to a frown. "She hasn't been causing you any problems, has she?"
Quentin shook his head.

"She's not in any trouble?" Shona almost held her breath.

"No, definitely not." Quentin shook his head again, surprised when she exhaled noisily. "I'm sorry Shona, I didn't mean to worry you."

"That's fine." She smiled at him, beckoning him to sit down and she sat opposite him. "Oh Quentin, I'm sorry, where are my manners? Would you like tea, or coffee, or anything?" She got straight to her feet again.

"I'm fine thank you, no need to do anything special."

"Okay." She sat down again.
They locked eyes and in the silence, weighed each other up. "Ursula told me about your... History." He settled on. "You'll probably be aware of my... Erm.."

"History?" She smiled at him, using his word.
Quentin actually laughed. "Yes, let's say that." He cleared his throat. "I don't know, I mean, it's not my place to say, but, you know, if you need anything, anyone, any help." Grimacing, he stopped. "That came out all wrong." He explained.

"Oh, you are sweet." She grinned at him. "I know what you are trying to say, at least I think I do."

"You do?" His eyebrows raised sharply.

"If I need a man, then I can call you. Likewise, if you need a woman, you can call me." She blushed at how outright she was speaking. "You know, for events and... things."

"I know what you mean." He too beamed. "Thank you, Shona. I have told myself that I'd never look at another woman, but sometimes I wonder if I'm missing out." He confessed. Seeing her shock, he continued. "Forgive me for speaking out of turn. Ursula and her talk of relationships has gotten into my head. She wants only for you to be as happy as she is - and she wants the same for me."

A lump came into Shona's throat. "She said that?"

He nodded, and laughed at himself. "I don't know why I had to come and tell you, but I thought I should. Thank you for hearing me out." He got to his feet then.

"Thank you for telling me." She met him at the door to the shop; they both reached for the handle at the same time. "You didn't have to. I mean," she kicked herself. "It's hard this life and romance thing, isn't it?" She too laughed at herself. "It's so easy in the books and movies."

He smiled, his smile one of relief. "A lot of life is."

Hesitating, she thought he was going to kiss her. She wanted in that instant to kiss him. But the moment passed as a customer was trying to make their way inside the shop. Quentin held the door open for her customer, exchanged pleasantries and with a smile for her, left.

Shona didn't know whether to be grateful or sad that he'd gone.

Together as promised to discuss the natural beauty of the island and how to enhance it to satisfy everyone, with minimal disruption to the Treduggan family, the trio of Yves, Caitlin and Kim sat down at the large table at Harbourtown Inn.

The pair were between the morning and afternoon tours, and Kim likewise had some free time. It had, however, taken weeks to get to this stage. Much as he'd struggled to get the right time with Nolan for his supplementary training; Yves sighed. He looked up as Caitlin squeezed his hand under the table.

"Are you alright?" She asked him.

"I'm fine. So much to do, so little time." He explained.

"A feeling I know well." Kim nodded. "Which is exactly why I wanted to propose that I undertake the majority of the work. It will ensure that our family is disturbed as little as possible, and we don't disrupt the RNLI's work," he recalled the RNLI hovercraft was kept on that side of the island at the last moment, "and everything is kept under control."

Looking at Caitlin, he continued.

"Your work also with the tours must not be interrupted." He smiled. "You are becoming well known in the business. I see that Cornish Birding has a regular spot set up for sightings here. Congratulations."

Caitlin blushed at the praise.

"It is another reason why we have been contacted by the Cornwall Tourist Office."

Caitlin and Yves leant forward in their seats. "They have?" They both spoke together.

"A request to make a recording for the next season has been granted. I would hope to have both of you included." He paused while they took the news in, grinning at each other. "I suggest that you get in touch with this man. I understand he is somewhat of a legend in birder circles."

Caitlin and Yves both knew the name of the man's photo in front of them - Mr Justin Thyme. They both gasped - he was indeed a legend. Getting an acknowledgement of what they were doing for Harbourtown by Mr Thyme would skyrocket the business.

"I'm sure he would travel across from the Isles of Scilly to take a talk." Kim was beaming at their shocked and excited expressions. "Let me know if you need anything to sweeten the deal, but I doubt it will be necessary. Once he has heard what is happening here he will be itching to get involved, as we all are."

Gauging their excitement, he plunged forward with more good news.

"The mudflats are a perfect area for cultivating into a wildlife habitat, such as an estuary or swamp." Kim began. "With the sea water providing a regular flush when the tide rises, it would make a perfect area. With careful planning, it would soon evolve."

Yves and Caitlin were staring at him wide-eyed.

"You really think it can be done?" Yves was first to find his voice.

"I'm sure that it would not be too difficult a task. The hardest part is done by Mother Nature herself." He shrugged. "This could provide us with a prime location for oyster beds, as well as a premium site for waders and ducks, and fish."

"Oysters?" Caitlin gasped.

"How much space are we talking about here?" Yves had a feeling that Kim had not only done the research but also knew how successful the venture could turn out to be.

"Enough." Kim smiled at him. "More than enough, in fact."

"Harbourtown could also become known as the place for oysters in this area?" Caitlin still couldn't believe her ears.

"It would take five years for the first batch to be ready. This is not a quick process." He warned them. "I had been thinking about it all for a while now, but I never had anyone to listen to my mad ideas."

Caitlin felt a touch of sympathy for him. She looked at Yves and knew her partner was thinking the same.

"Your ideas are far from mad." Yves told him.

Caitlin nodded her agreement. "What else do you have planned?" She was sitting on the edge of her seat now, in trepidation.

"Oh no," Kim laughed, "you wouldn't want to know."

All of a sudden the atmosphere between them had changed.

"Well," Yves began, "anytime you want to talk, or you want someone to bounce ideas off, let us know."

Kim looked up at them in surprise. "Really?"

"Really." They both spoke together, sharing a smile.

Chapter 27

When Oxander discovered that Ursula had many admirers, he reacted furiously! Storming over to the shop to have it out with her, he didn't care who else was around. Once he'd fallen for her, he had lost his heart and wanted her to himself.

Pulling her to one side he demanded that she never looked at another man if she really wanted to be with him. She told him not to be so ridiculous and walked away, expecting him to leave. Instead he stayed and watched her being particularly flirty with the tourists in order to entice them to spend more money.

"Stop it, Ursula!" His words echoed around the place, causing everyone to look round. "Can't you just be happy with me? Do you have to seduce every man on the island!" Slamming the door behind him in a huff, the atmosphere was so tense you could cut it with a knife.

Ursula didn't know what to say.

"Wow, someone is a bit uptight this morning." Alicia tried to break the awkward silence.

"He's very Jekyll and Hyde, isn't he?" Eddie commented. "A few weeks ago he was practically begging anyone who would listen to keep you away from him." He rolled his eyes. "Show's over folks, sorry about that. Don't worry, entertainment is free." He joked, getting everyone in the room to at least smile and likewise dispersing the awful atmosphere.

Ursula gave him a thankful smile.

As Nolan drew into the harbour and moored his boat into the usual spot, he saw Oxander making his way along the cobbled quayside to him. His attention was redirected by the now usual group of seals gathered around his boat, bobbing hopefully in the water as if surrounding him until he gave them some fish.

"You guys really need to learn how to pay your way." He laughed, tossing in some of that morning's catch for them. They were so regular, he now kept some back for them after his paying customers were happy to choose the best bits. "Enjoy it!"

"Nolan!" Oxander still walked with a limp after his accident, but that didn't stop him bearing down on the young fisherman.

When he looked up, Nolan found Oxander right above him on the quay. He wondered what prompted a rare visit from the harbourmaster.

"Morning Oxander, I hope you are well." He began.

"You cheeky bugger."

Nolan spluttered. "I was merely asking you a polite question most people reserve for this time in the morning." He tried to joke, but Oxander was in no mood to laugh.

Crossing his arms in front of his chest, Oxander launched into a tirade.

Nolan's mouth fell open. "What's got into you?" His voice was amazed.

"You!"

"Me?" Nolan repeated.

"Or rather you got into Ursula, didn't you? I'll bet it was your smart mouth that talked your way into..."

"Stop right there!"

It was Oxander's turn for his mouth to drop open in shock. How dare Nolan cut him off!

"Don't you dare smear my reputation, and Ursula's, without knowing the facts. We went on a few dates, we kissed, we did not join in a blissful union and we are not together now. Not that it is any of your business."

Oxander didn't know what to say.

"Did you hear me over your own self importance?" Nolan snarled. He dismounted from his boat and stood on the quay nose to nose with Oxander. "I'm waiting for my apology. Start whenever you want." He too crossed his arms in front of his chest, striking a battle pose. "Then, if you were half decent, you'd also apologise to Ursula for what you said."

"You're so full of yourself." Oxander snarled back at him, pushing him away. Nolan took a few steps backwards from the force of the shove. "I'm not apologising to anyone for anything." Oxander continued, shoving him harder.

As the argument had started and Nolan had left his boat to confront Oxander, Yves had smoothly pulled up at the harbour in his boat, in preparation to switch over into the hovercraft. Seeing the two men, his intuition was alerted to the threatening tone of their conversation. He didn't know why, or what had been said, and he wasn't entirely sure that he should get involved.

He exclaimed in horror as Oxander pushed Nolan off the quay and into the water, narrowly avoiding hitting his head as he plummeted in. Turning the boat around, Yves was soon at Nolan's side; hoisting him over the edge of the boat with his boat hook. In those precious seconds, Oxander had turned and walked back to the lighthouse, disappearing from sight.

"What was that about?" A voice asked, as the two men alighted at the harbour once more.

Looking up, they saw Kim on the fringe of the gathered crowd. He had been the one to speak. Everyone praised Yves's fast reflexes, and they were all concerned about Nolan.

"RNLI training is so ingrained it was sheer instinct." Yves half joked.

"Thank you." Nolan told him. "I wasn't going to drown, but getting up unaided would've been a bit awkward." Despite himself, he shivered. "He started on me the minute he saw I'd docked."

"Not two minutes ago, he caused a scene here." Tanya was amongst the crowd, coming forward with a scratchy wool blanket to drape around Nolan's shoulders.

Both Nolan and Yves looked at her. "He did?" They both said together.

"Is everything okay?" Kim continued, his frown matching theirs.

"It sounds like Quentin has given him something that has caused him to lose his mind." Eddie commented. "Are you sure you're okay?" He checked with Nolan. "I was convinced you'd hit your head as you fell." He shuddered.

"Must've missed the wall by a hair." Nolan too shuddered. The crowd shook their heads.

"You should come in and dry off, and have a stiff drink." David took Nolan by the shoulders, steering him towards the Inn. "Thank goodness you weren't hurt. It's not exactly cold out, but come in and sit by the fire."

Murmurs of agreement reached them, and the crowd followed the pair inside, leaving Yves and Kim alone.

"This will not go unnoticed." Kim began.

"While I agree," Yves nodded, "let me ask Quentin a few questions about this. Maybe Eddie has a point."

"That's fine, but it makes no difference. He will need to be dealt with." Kim's tone was still angry.

"Don't take this the wrong way, but don't tackle him alone. At least have Quentin or myself with you." He saw Kim raise his eyebrows. "I'd not forgive myself if he snapped again and something happened to you."

"He wouldn't dare!" Kim thundered. "He will not get away with this, I assure you."

"I don't doubt it." Yves said. "Are you going in?" He jerked his thumb towards the Inn. "I need to get going. I'm already late for picking up the next group."

"Yes, you go. I'll still be here when you get back." Kim replied.

Yves wasn't sure if that was a statement or a threat.

Chapter 28

Yves had of course worried about Nolan after witnessing that scene on the harbour; Caitlin, when she found out, was worried about Ursula. Oxander was known to be headstrong and stubborn at times, but he'd never before shown any violent tendencies.

This uncharacteristic temper tantrum of his had come from somewhere though. She hoped it was a one off, not wanting the atmosphere of Harbourtown ruined, both for personal and professional reasons. Kim would sort it out, she found herself relieved to have the thought.

Kim positively bellowed from the bottom of the lighthouse steps. "Oxander! Get down here at once!"

Vimto had been in his usual spot overlooking the harbour when Oxander had returned from his rampage. The humans were all behaving weirdly today - some even more than normal! Looking across at Oxander, he saw him grimace and get to his feet. Following his back as he retreated down the steps, Vimto began to wash himself as he usually did at this time of the day. He wondered how much arguing would ensue.

"Your antics are immature and irresponsible!" Kim began, once he saw Oxander's feet on the steps above his head.

Having followed the noise of his footsteps as he followed the steps downwards, Kim knew he was on the way down to see him as requested. Waiting until he arrived before continuing, he allowed the atmosphere between them to stifle.

"I was prepared to give you the benefit of the doubt over the incident in the café and shop, but I cannot condone the downright dangerous stunt you pulled on the quay. What in

God's name were you thinking?"

Oxander virtually sulked. This only intensified Kim's anger.

"If you had caused him serious harm, I would have been forced to have you charged. You do realise that, don't you?"

Oxander kept up his silence.

"Whether you want to or not, you will apologise publicly to Nolan - now!"

"But..." He began.

Kim cut him off. "But nothing! Find him, and make sure you say it like you mean it. I want to hear no more about your or your behaviour, or you will be on the next boat back to Conning. Do I make myself clear?"

Oxander crossed his arms in front of him. He almost smiled. "You can't do that. I'm needed here."

"Don't you dare undermine my authority!" Kim's face was turning puce with rage. "Although the smooth running of the harbour business is done efficiently, you were easily replaced while you convalesced. It would do you good to remember that!"

Oxander visibly quailed. In fact, he hadn't thought of it like that - and he hadn't thought that anyone else had either.

"Well, what are you waiting for? Go!" Kim almost pushed him in the direction of the harbour.

He remained where he was by the lighthouse watching, as Oxander made his way across to the village, into the Inn. He disappeared only for several minutes before coming back out again to return to the lighthouse. All in all, it had taken a mere twelve minutes; ten of those had been the walk there and back.

"I trust that you are fit to do your duties and there will not be any more trouble." Kim warned.

"Yes, Kim. Sorry." Oxander spoke meekly. He'd been shocked when he saw that Kim had not only watched but waited for him, and knew that the discussion was far from over.

"I hope your apology to Nolan was more sincere than that." Backed into a corner, theoretically speaking, Oxander nodded. He dared not verbally reply, in fear of receiving another volley of displeasure.

"Good. Now get back to work. I don't want to hear anymore about your behaviour from anyone." Kim pointed to the lighthouse and Oxander knew that he wouldn't leave until he had returned to the top observation window.

Grudgingly, he took to the steps once more, the extra journey causing his injuries to throb. Taking more pills when he was alone - he'd watched Kim's retreating back so that he knew he was safe to breathe - he realised that Vimto too had left.

Not that he had any control over the whereabouts of the animal, even if people did think the cat was his. He sighed. Over time, he'd found that Vimto was a very good listener and he often sought solace in telling the cat his human woes.

Perhaps this meant that the animal was his after all... Although, wasn't the saying that you never owned a cat, but it owned you?

Was it simply a medication issue or was there actually something wrong with Oxander's state of mind? Quentin puzzled over what he'd been told by Yves during the call, and decided to cut short his afternoon surgery to see Oxander sooner rather than later.

He had known that it was too soon for him to be making his return, but even as the words left his mouth, Quentin knew Oxander wasn't listening. As far as he was concerned, the bones had knitted together well and so, healing was over with. There was nothing to stop him returning, and equalling nothing to be gained from staying away much longer.

The residual headache was a temporary issue, Quentin informed him, half hiding his own doubts. The prescription of painkillers and muscle relaxants aided Oxander's return to his normal life, although he would likely need them for quite a while yet. That had been another point that they'd argued over - Oxander was ready to go without the drugs, but Quentin had managed to talk him into keeping a supply in case he needed any.

Now Quentin wondered if the anger issues were a side effect - if so, he was partly to blame for what had happened in his patient's brain. This thought caused him to make the short journey even quicker. He found Oxander in a very solemn and untalkative mood. Their conversation was stilted and awkward, and soon Oxander sent him away without so much as a thank you for coming. That was typical of Oxander!

Calling at the Inn on the way back to check on what had happened from the other side of the story, he discovered why Oxander was more antsy than usual. Kim's bellowing had echoed around the village; the complete opposite to how quietly Oxander's apology had been inside the premises.

Everybody had heard what had happened since the incident on the quayside, and yet nobody felt sorry for Oxander. It seemed, Quentin smiled with the thought, the tide had turned against the harbourmaster.

The fallout between Nolan and Oxander over Ursula triggered memories Quentin would have rather remained buried in the back of his mind forever. The pain of a double heartbreak, on top of not having his beloved give her heart to him on what should have been the best day of their lives had sent his romantic inclinations into a very dark and distant place.

Swearing to remain a bachelor for the rest of his days, he vowed not to let another woman steal a moment further of his time. It had been an eye opening experience to be with Ursula for those journeys to and from her visits to Quentin, and he did wonder - at times, albeit briefly - if he was losing a great potential partner in a quieter, more mature lady.

Someone like Shona - the complete opposite of bold, flirtatious Ursula; not interested in how much attention they can draw, nor being in with the crowd. Someone happy to help out whenever they were needed and not required to have anything in return. Someone to celebrate others' successes as their own. Someone to fall into an easy life rhythm with; to be comfortable with and never feel unloved, unwelcome or unwanted.

He harrumphed with his thoughts. Qualities like that were for someone who plainly didn't exist. He certainly wouldn't be fighting for a woman's hand as Nolan and Oxander had - if she didn't want him to be exclusively hers, and vice versa, then it was a relationship without a future.

But he had to be fair to Nolan, the relationship he had with Ursula had run its course, and Oxander was getting the wrong end of the stick because he was blinded by his jealousy. It was little wonder really that so many books and songs told tales of woe in love and war.

He sighed.

Chapter 29

All of a sudden there was a mad fluttering as every bird on the island disappeared into hiding. Some of the birders were confused by this bizarre behaviour, but most knew it meant that bad weather was on the way.

Caitlin certainly did, cutting short their visit to the islands in order to head back as soon as possible. Fortunately the journey back was a short one, and by engaging the motor, it would be a fast one. Usually she didn't have the motor running between the islands and when they were what she considered close, because she didn't want to disturb their quarry.

Black ominous looking clouds rolled in above their heads. She swore under her breath. Would the storm be faster than them? At the harbour, they docked and all ran for the protection of the Inn. Slipping and sliding on the wet cobbles as they ran, luckily everyone stayed on their feet. Caitlin had never been so relieved to get inside!

The wind howled, the sun disappeared behind the clouds, the temperature suddenly dropped 15 degrees and then the rain started - huge fat water droplets that bounced off the cobbles, soaking everything it touched. Proper rain, someone joked. A few shrieks were uttered as the lightning struck not far away from them and thunder rumbled above the rooftop.

"No need to worry, it's safe here." David soothed his customer's ruffled nerves. "We even have our own generator in case of a power outage."

Caitlin gave him a thankful smile. "We should action Plan W." She told him.

The birder nearest her queried the name.

"Plan Wet." She elaborated, shrugging at the simplicity. "No need to be all high tech and use big words." She laughed.

The group laughed with her, but their collective attention wavered back to the window as another streak of lightning flashed through the sky.

"I'd hate to be in the lighthouse during a storm." One of the group said, shivering. "Isn't it terribly unsafe up there?"

"No, that was planned for." Caitlin informed them. "At the very top, there's a lightning rod in case lightning strikes the lighthouse."

"And the cat?" Someone else asked, looking around the room.

"He'll be in there too, or at least somewhere in the warm and dry." Another responded. "Animals aren't stupid, they know when the bad stuff is coming and go into hiding."

"Bloody clever!" Several people exclaimed.

"But how do they know?" One person asked.

"They are extra sensitive to the changing pressures." Someone else piped up. "They can't read the rain radar."

Hoots of laughter echoed around the Inn.

Vimto was in the warm and dry, up in the lighthouse. As much as he wanted to go out for his afternoon stroll - it was becoming increasingly lucrative day by day as more people offered him treats - he was not going out in *that*. No animal would, not even the daftest human would.

Slipping and sliding on the treacherous cobblestoned quayside of the harbour as they desperately dashed for cover, the last of the humans disappeared from view. The beacon from the lighthouse started to flash, warning all who saw it.

Out of the corner of his eye, he saw two figures in waterproofs below. They were pushing each other; any noises were drowned out by the thunder overhead.

Something glinted in the flash of lightning above them: in the next moment, one figure slumped to the ground and the other ran off. Another lightning flash and gust of wind displayed the face of the human fleeing the scene: it was one Vimto recognised well.

It was an age before anyone came out of the Inn. When they did, it was the tour group under Caitlin's wing - they all piled into the hovercraft and Caitlin and Yves took off, taking them back to the mainland. Nobody looked over at the lighthouse; nobody saw the figure. Despite the weather becoming calmer, nobody else appeared for what seemed like an eternity.

All that waiting and watching had been a complete waste of time, Vimto thought, beginning to clean and preen so when he arrived for his treats he would look his best.

Oxander raised the alarm, seeing the body lying there after the storm from the observation deck of the lighthouse. Even his usual unruffled character prevented him from doing or saying much between calling for help and it arriving in the form of Quentin and Walter. He stood warily on the quayside, not allowing anyone near the body.

Although he knew Quentin's remarkable doctoring skills were beyond the casualty, it still shocked him when Quentin pulled the blanket over the body, covering it completely.

A silence fell over the assembled crowd and Vimto, watching from the shadows of the harbour wall nearby, felt the sorrow. Ruling Ursula's death as accidental, the indent on the back of her head the obvious cause, Quentin presumed that she had slipped, striking her head on the cobbled quayside - that would have killed her outright.

His common sense theory was one that most people shared: no signs of a struggle, no witnesses, and with nothing around her that could have been used as a potential weapon, there was to suggest otherwise. After the ferocity of the storm even the bloodstain had been washed away, leaving only a minimal mark.

Quentin had Walter take over: arrangements needed to be made to send the body to the mainland morgue. The second time this year! He felt upset because it was such a waste of life.

Walter lamented that he'd never see her or feel her love again; Oxander was speechless, his face deathly white; Nolan shook his head, tears running down his cheeks. Nobody could believe what they'd seen.

Quentin did his best to console the crowd, but was glad when David took over, steering his wife and Eddie and Alicia back to the Inn to look after them, telling him and Walter that he would break the news to Shona.

Poor Shona! Quentin felt deeply sorry for her; not envying them of the task of telling her. What a terrible accident! Half of him wanted to go to her, but half of him didn't. He wasn't sure how receptive she'd been to his arrival in the wake of such tragic news.

The whole island was in shock. Lots of drinkers at the Inn stayed longer than usual that night and ordered more than usual in an attempt to dull their pain. Nolan and Walter were two such drinkers, and when Oxander arrived wearing a miserable expression he made three.

Not long after this, Vimto waltzed into the Inn as usual, lifting the gloomy atmosphere with his presence. He looked around for the young blonde woman who usually fussed over him the most - not finding her, he was perplexed: not even showing Oxander recognition as he slunk out again.

"My God, even the cat knows!" Walter said in disbelief.

Chapter 30

Despite the cause of death ruled as an accident, it was ruled that a post mortem would be required. Having no previous experience with this sort of thing, Shona didn't argue.

Because of the strangeness of the story Ursula told her, over time, and when probed, about her damaged relations with the rest of the family, she agonised over contacting any of them.

However, it wasn't right that her parents would hear it from the newspapers, that was true. Neither was it right that Ursula's parents found out that way, but she didn't have details for everyone. Instead plumping for the general option of calling home, she relayed what had happened to the first person who picked up the phone and sat down, expecting a long and difficult conversation. Possibly one that she would have to go through multiple times...

Eventually the coroner's office informed them that Ursula's death hadn't been caused by a blow to the back of the head by a large flat object - a cobblestone, as Quentin suspected - but actually something much sharper and narrower.

A cast was made of the strange mark, and once shown to Walter, he straight away identified it as the head of a boat hook. There was no mistaking it, the indent was perfectly shaped like a boathook.

Speaking in turns with Walter and Quentin, the police had no option but to reassign the case as a murder investigation. Walter almost had a nervous breakdown - a murder on his patch! Never in his worst nightmares had anything like this happened.

Worse, his Ursula had been taken from him needlessly! He vowed to bring the killer to justice and to seek some kind of revenge while doing so... Legally or otherwise.

After relaying the dreadful news to their family members, Shona wondered where to begin in order to plan the funeral. She didn't even know how long it would be until they would release the body for the service.

The small chapel in Conning would be the nearest place to have the... It was a ceremony of sorts, she assumed. The vicar had been very kind to her, and asked her the necessary questions gently. Much to Shona's dismay she could answer very few of them, as never had either her or Ursula even thought to have a conversation about what most normal people viewed as a morbid topic.

The options for burial or cremation were open. Shona had no idea what Ursula would have wanted, and she could seek no help from any of their family. So, she did what she thought was best in the circumstances - she took a guess, using what she would have liked as a guide.

The vicar seemed to agree with that plan. That left only one issue - costs for the funeral. Shona's small amount of savings had been ploughed into the new shop, along with money from her previous home, so she could ill afford the basics, never mind any additional costs a funeral and wake would incur.

Sighing, she knew it meant another call to the family to hopefully resolve the problem. Then when the event had passed and she could put the whole sorry episode behind her, Shona could return to her quiet life.

For the last week, Vimto had made a daily pilgrimage to the village, stopping off at the Inn, the shop and the café, always as if he was looking out for Ursula. He saw various people at various times lay flowers at the same spot he'd seen the figure sink to the cobbles.

By the end of the week, when he saw Shona there and a photo of Ursula was pinned by the tributes, he knew it was for his friend. The truth of what he'd seen during the storm from his position in the lighthouse registered in his brain.

On his next visit to the Inn, Oxander, Nolan and Walter were sitting together, and Vimto as usual went across to Nolan. He tolerated Walter but Nolan he felt was somehow special - like Ursula had been.

As Oxander reached out for him, he backed up, glaring at him, eyes narrowed.

"What's got into him?" Walter found his voice.

Oxander shrugged.

"Have you upset him? Didn't you feed him or something?" Nolan questioned.

Oxander rolled his eyes. "It wouldn't matter if I didn't feed him, as many other people do. He should be too fat to climb the lighthouse steps by now. You're thoroughly spoiled, aren't you." He told Vimto.

Tail held upright, ears pinned back, Vimto growled. He held Oxander's stare for a while, before leaving defiantly.

That evening, people talked about the weirdness of the cat's attitude. Eventually, the harbourmaster joked that he thought it was bad enough that fate was against him, but now even the cat has turned against him - another round is bought much to everyone's delight and so they laughed at the joke, consoling Oxander.

Beyond relieved to have an amount forwarded to her that more than paid the costs involved, Shona was gobsmacked to receive a lump sum in place of Ursula's inheritance from her estranged family.

Because her father had married Ursula's mother when they were both in their fifties, the two women had been thrown together relatively late in their lives - Ursula had been 17 when the marriage had taken place; that same year, Shona turned 25. As polite, Shona had left her Cornish home to travel north for the wedding and used the rather long commute home as an excuse to not stay for longer than necessary.

Therefore, she had seen her step-mother and step-sister only at a few family gatherings. The same travelling distance and time excuse stood her in good stead over the years, she found. Until Ursula turned up on her doorstep two years ago, she hadn't known much about her beyond the small amount of courtesy conversations they'd shared.

Shona's kind-heartedness registered that Ursula came to her because she knew there she was safe - and also that she knew Shona wouldn't let her down. Shona believed in treating people with the respect she herself wanted from others. It was a sad fact that in today's world this didn't always happen. Down here in this part of Cornwall, she found the people on the whole much friendlier and happier than in the larger cities.

First of all, she tried to refuse the inheritance, but her protests were waved away. With the arrangements taken care of by the Conning vicar, Shona next considered her windfall. She wanted to make the most of it - and even after a sizable donation in Ursula's name to the church, she still had enough to invest in her own business, if she so desired.

That was a thought!

The replacement shop by the pub wasn't ideal, but it was in the best available location she'd had to admit when she and Ursula had been offered it. There was no room for extension or expansion, however.

It struck her that setting up an RNLI lifeboat shop would be a great way to give back, both to the local community and the lifesaving charity, but where could such premises be located - and who would run it?

At the next area meeting on the mainland, she decided she would put the idea out amongst the local people, and go on from there.

Chapter 31

News of the Harbourtown Murder spread far and wide - beginning to also affect business in Harbourtown and the Islands, even spreading through to Conning.

On the quayside, people laid flowers and wreaths where Ursula had been found. The torrential rain had washed away any potential clues there may have been at the scene, so Walter was at a loss for where to start.

If nobody had been out with her, and everyone had been sheltering from the storm as they always did, everyone would have an alibi. Nonetheless, the truth remained that a murderer lived amongst them.

Fear and frustration gripped him, churning Walter's stomach.

When the next few groups of birders cancelled because of the recent deaths, frustration amongst the villagers rose. The upcoming bookings at Roundhouse too are cancelled at short notice, because nobody wants to be anywhere near the supposed doomed island. Talk resurfaces about Roger's death and rumours fly - the words curse and jinx are mentioned several times.

The worst news came when cargo ships refused to continue using Harbourtown, rerouting to Falmouth and St Ives instead. Something needed to be done before the place became a ghost town.

The Police Commissioner summoned Walter to his office on the mainland.

After the humiliation of the meeting with the Commissioner, Walter's mood sank even lower. An arsonist and two deaths, all in one year!

The blame lay squarely at his door, the Commissioner told him. He was too lax, too predictable, not visible enough and not proactive enough. If good policemen weren't so hard to find, he would be fired.

Walter didn't know that this meeting had been orchestrated to spur him into action; he took every word personally and wanted to tender his resignation on the spot.

Nodding at what he was told - an Inspector was coming to help them clear up the mess at Harbourtown so that the village could resume business as soon as humanly possible - he was told to take some time off to gather himself. But not too much; he shouldn't wallow or lose himself in his grief.

The Commissioner told him that he would be expected to work alongside the visiting Inspector, but Walter had tuned out of the conversation, the same thought on a loop in his head that he was a useless policeman and the troubles were all his fault.

Usually he enjoyed a pint of ale at The Empty Tankard before heading home for the evening; but something took him back to his boat and back across the water to Harbourtown. His feet dragged him into the Inn and to a quiet seat in the corner.

He thanked David when he approached with a pint ready for him; refusing the offer to talk and nodding his promise that if he wanted anything, he'd ask.

Walter could no longer think.

Chatter in both pubs, Harbourtown Inn and The Empty Tankard, was the same. Who had murdered Ursula? And why? The general consensus was of shock - this was a quiet part of the country where there hadn't been violence in the past. Where would it end? What was the world coming to?

"That investigator,"

"Inspector," someone interrupted.

"That investigator inspector will be questioning everyone, and our Walter has already done that, so what does he think he'll find?"

"He'll find the truth." Isaac put in.

Lots of their patrons gaped at him.

"Every murder mystery is the same." Cecillia added. "Nobody outright admits they did it, do they?"

Isaac, and a few others, nodded.

"Poor Walter isn't taking it well." Someone else said.

"Can you blame him? He had his eye on Ursula, and she's gone. Now he's been hauled up in front of the Police Commissioner. He'll probably lose his job."

"No!" Several gasps arose.

"Surely not?"

Lots of sighing and shrugging went on.

It was much the same at Harbourtown Inn. David and Tanya were both present behind the bar. Walter was tucked into a corner, his attention not even in the room on his drink.

"Poor Walter," the whisper went around the place.

"The Inspector is well versed in things like this." Tanya began. "That's why he's been called in to help solve the murder. It's no reflection on Walter." She spoke deliberately louder than normal so that Walter could hear.

"What we need to do is to work together." David agreed. "Flush out the villain and get our lives back."

There were several 'hear, hear' murmurs of agreement.

Walter groaned. "Nothing will bring her back."

All eyes went to David and Tanya.

"We know, but we can't show her, and Shona, disrespect by giving up." Tanya made her way through the crowd to him.

She placed her hand gently on his shoulder. "Someone, somewhere, knows the truth. It will come right."

Walter looked up at her. "You really think so?" His voice was flat.

"Yes." Tanya pulled a smile to her face. Looking around, she saw several nods in the crowd.

Walter's gaze returned to his drink.

Chapter 32

"Characters, Venus, every single one of them." The Superintendent leaned so far back in the office chair it squeaked violently and shook, but held.

Silently Inspector Venus was thankful: not because he didn't want his superior to hurt himself but because he would have incurred his wrath when he laughed at his plight.

Characters. Venus raised one eyebrow quizzically. In the property business, character was the word they used often for small and cramped otherwise unsaleable properties, mostly buildings that were also old and damp and needing a multitude of repair work in order to be remotely habitable.

"Characters, Sir?" He invited the Superintendent to clarify the word.

"A bunch of nitwits, misfits and eejits." He smiled at his Inspector's obvious dismay. "Write that down to use in your next book. Bah-ha-ha-ha!" He paused. "You can have that one, no need to credit me."

"Um, thank you Sir?" Venus ventured.

"Now off you go. Time waits for no man."

"Yes Sir." Venus escaped from the office as fast as possible.

Before leaving for Harbourtown, he asked for the case details to review. Initially, he had wondered why there wasn't a file for him when the Superintendent informed him of the case. Dismayed to find no report on file from the local man, Walter Copper, Venus began to ask questions.

Most of his colleagues stated Walter was a proper old fashioned policeman, but he'd been hit hard by the murder - professionally and personally. Venus sighed. No wonder he was of little use!

Walter would assist him in finding the murderer, he was told, but that was only part of Venus's responsibility at

Harbourtown.

Walter was waiting for Inspector Venus as the hovercraft docked, or whatever it did, at Harbourtown. Touching the brim of his hat respectfully, he nodded a hello at the Inspector. Instantly, Venus offered his heartfelt condolences, vowing to have the murderer caught and justice served.

Walter grew several inches in stature with those words. He allowed himself to think for the first time that perhaps having the Inspector's help was a good idea, and not a blemish on his copybook.

Escorting the Inspector across the cobblestone quay to the Inn, and when inside, through to one of the back rooms where his small office was located. There, they could talk privately, Walter promised. This was the office of the Inn on Harbourtown and Venus wondered what the significance of this was. It would come out in time, he knew; these things always did.

Politely he introduced David and Tanya; they insisted on being called by their christian names, although the Inspector started off using their formal names. Everyone on Harbourtown used their first names as it was friendlier, Venus was informed. He raised his eyebrows.

Firstly, Walter gave a basic rundown of the tragic night in question, his voice breaking when he told of his arrival and saw the blanket over the victim. In his thirty odd years on this beat, he'd never encountered a murder victim - he had only seen a few who had died, including a local fisherman several months previously.

In an effort to aid him in keeping his composure, Venus questioned him on what had happened to the fisherman - specifically the cause of death and the circumstances around it.

Walter went into automated mode, detailing the incident.

"Do you think the two deaths are related?" The Inspector asked after Walter had finished verbalising his report.

Walter's eyes widened; obviously this was a new thought for him. Venus nodded to himself, having wondered if there was a link between the seemingly separate cases.

"I hadn't thought of that." Walter confessed. "Storms wreak havoc on anyone out in them, and Roger was unlucky to fall prey to the lightning attack." As he hesitated, Venus knew something of value was forthcoming. "There had been rumours, in the village, and it was true that Roger was unlikely to have been out in his boat by choice in such weather."

"Village?" Venus queried.

"We refer to Harbourtown as a village." Walter clarified. "It certainly has that air to it, with only four people on the hill, plus the rest down here in the harbour area."

"Hmm…" Venus made a few notes after encouraging Walter to supply him with names and basics about the person, or persons, the rumours circled around. "What did the post mortem show?"

Walter swallowed hard. "There wasn't one, and it can't be done posthumously - he was cremated before his ashes were scattered at sea." He added, breaking down then. "Roger was my best friend." He managed to choke out.

Venus was well aware that Walter was too close to the case - to both cases really. Usually in this situation, a policeman would be removed from the case, but this was by no means a usual case. Their work would be cut out if they were to discover the truth.

Switching his thinking to the list of the people he would have to interview gave Walter time to gather himself. It would be interesting to question the attending doctor, Venus mused, and the younger fisherman. The second man, Nolan, was the victim of the villagers' rumours - and incidentally the ex-boyfriend of the murder victim. That was very interesting indeed!

Could it be a coincidence?

There were lots of preliminary interviews to undertake, Inspector Venus discovered as Walter informed him of the potential list of suspects. This much information necessitated a list:

The lifeguards at Bountiful Bay - Marissa, Will and Dwayde.

Hope, Joy and Faith Anchorage run the arty Roundhouse Island. All cousins.

Various 'villagers' who are only really seen at the Inn - retirees, of whom there are four, all unrelated. Mr Mustard, Mr Boxer, Mr Plummer and Mr Halfpenny.

The Treduggan family and their adopted son, Kim Oke. Kim is involved with the running of Harbourtown although the harbourmaster/lighthouse keeper has the job of running the harbour.

K Oke.

Alicia Cakebread - the café owner. Eddie Clare - partner of Alicia, a baker.

A Cakebread and E Clare.

Isaac Saw - newly married to Cecillia Saw, runs The Empty

Tankard pub in Conning, which used to be owned by David and Tanya. Son of David and Tanya.
  I Saw and C Saw.

Quentin Farma - the local doctor.
  Q Farma

Oxander Knowe - the harbourmaster.
  O Knowe.

Nolan Keel and Roger Shoal are the fishermen.
  Shoal and Keel.

David Tale and Tanya Hirst - innkeeper and his wife.
  D Tale and T Hirst.

Caitlin Gardiner runs the birders tours and Treduggan's gardener. Partner Yves Aske - handyman/ ferryman.
  C Gardiner. Y Aske.

Shona Tate - ran the shop in Conning with younger step-sister, Ursula Watt, until Ursula moved across to Harbourtown.
  S Tate. U Watt.

Bird watchers (15) - included ornologists Leslie Swann, Bryony Wilde, Victor Nestor, George Reed, Zee Flocke.
  B Wilde, G Reed.

Birders - Rick Turpin, Tom Johnson, Nigel Taylor, Sam Jones, William Hill, Harry Cane, Charles King, Ken Newton, Simon Baker and Tom Ford.

- Does everyone have a name that either dictates their profession or sounds weird when you use their first initial?! Venus wondered to himself if this was his inner writer making assumptions.

The local boats too had names, and the Inspector was careful to note these with their owners in case such information was valuable at a later date.

Oceanmaster is the ferryboat (hovercraft). Yves has the ferry boat but also, The Other Woman.
Fillet was Roger's fishing boat and Nolan's is called The Storm.
Lady Sybil is the policeman's boat.
The lifeboat is called Towednack.
Kernow Star belongs to the Treduggan family - usually piloted by Kim.

Seaton, Mermaid, Angarrack, Stithians and Tidehopper are casual sailboats of different sizes for general hire. Although Caitlin and Yves have Stithians on hire for tours and Tidehopper is hired permanently to the Roundhouse cousins, although none of them own a boat.

- isn't that a bit strange as there's no road access?! Venus noted.

Chapter 33

Could anyone be knocked off the list straight away, Venus mused. He had to keep in mind the fact that it was possible - albeit an outside chance - that Walter could be a suspect. Evidence otherwise pointed against it, but at this stage it was still possible, so his name still had to be on the list. However, Venus added it only mentally.

"So," he drew in a deep breath.

"Everyone has an alibi." Walter spoke up.

He'd remained quiet whilst the Inspector had compiled the lengthy list, adding bits where he thought it was necessary - and noticing that the Inspector had only written the facts, omitting most of his gossip.

"Water tight?" Venus raised his eyebrows with the joke.

Walter's impassive face didn't show that he even acknowledged the joke. "Everyone was together. We were at the Inn taking shelter from the storm. The Anchorage cousins were still on Roundhouse, as the lifeguards were at Bountiful Bay, so that takes them off the list as possibilities."

Consulting his notes, Venus didn't make a comment. "Everyone was at the Inn?"

"Not any of the Treduggans, of course. They were all at home together." Walter paused. "The mainlanders weren't at the Inn either. Oxander was in the lighthouse with Vimto. Quentin was at work in the surgery on the mainland."

Holding his hand up for Walter to stop, Venus repeated the name he hadn't heard mentioned before. "Vimto?"

Walter cracked a smile - the first one Venus had seen. "The cat."

"A cat?"

"The lighthouse cat. He was a stray who decided a while ago that he liked living here." Walter shrugged. "He also likes black olives and the local beer, given the chance."

A smile found its way to Venus's lips. "A beer drinking cat - is he the required legal age?"

Walter was glad to laugh. "The local brewery named it Salty Sea Dawg, as in the old nickname given to sailors. Ironic that a cat likes it."

"The beer that leaves it's patrons feline good, I suppose?" Venus joked, wondering why Walter was looking at him in shock.

"That's exactly what someone else said!" He explained. Shaking his head, he returned his thinking to the case. "It's a real stumper eh?" He said after a while, his expression changing back to one of sorrow and dismay.

"Someone is lying, that's obvious." Venus shook his head. "Same as in virtually every murder case. We need to ask ourselves who stood to gain the most from the act. Who had a motive?" He recalled some of the details Walter had given but hadn't been written down. "You said Shona, the step-sister, fell out with Ursula?"

Walter nodded. "When the job came up here, it made sense for Ursula to move to Harbourtown. Not long before that, they had to move premises on the mainland after an arson attack destroyed a row of shops, theirs included."

Venus's eyes widened. "Arson? I thought you said this was a quiet, law-abiding place?"

Walter didn't answer.

"The arsonist was caught, I assume?" Venus continued.

"When he tried to do the same again elsewhere." The local policeman confessed.

Reading between the lines, Venus sidestepped Walter's embarrassment tactfully. "Who else was affected by the fire?"

"The couple who run the café had a bakery there, Eddie

and Alicia." Walter spoke quickly. "I recommended to the Treduggans that they hire them for the café. It was a brilliant move."

Scanning the list in front of him, Venus found the couple in question - E Clare and A Cakebread. Those names had set him off on the unusual idea that mostly everyone's name stood for their profession, or their initials made weird reading that must have been beyond coincidence.

"They are a proper couple, not business partners?"

"Got engaged not so long ago." Walter smiled at the memory. "Perfectly suited."

Venus ignored the extra remark. "Nobody else?" Walter shook his head. "What about the innkeeper and his wife? Were they affected by the arson - did that bring them here?"

"No. They own The Empty Tankard over on the mainland. Once their son Isaac married Cecillia, they wanted a different challenge."

Venus snorted. "Not much difference - from a pub to an Inn."

"A different clientele." Walter argued back. "The Treduggans wanted David and Tanya because of their sterling reputation. Some people visit to sample the delights at the Inn; some come purely because it's run by David and Tanya." He shrugged. "The four retired bachelors on the island are regulars; they say it's the best place in the area - better than The Empty Tankard and that's award winning."

Venus's eyebrows raised again. "The Inn, the café, I suppose the lighthouse also is a tourist draw as well as a rather picturesque harbour. What else brings the tourists?"

"Only the birder tours. Treduggan house is private, but Caitlin, the gardener, offers bird watching wildlife tours. The gardens and woodland of the Treduggan property are included, before they all go out in a boat to the islands."

Venus almost laughed - Treduggan was another name

that sounded as if it couldn't have been made up, even in a fictional tale. If it had been used in one of Venus's books, no publisher would allow it because of the ridiculousness!

"You'd have thought the sound of the tourists in a boat would frighten off any wildlife, let alone birds. Birds are known to take flight easily." Venus thought aloud.

Walter again shrugged. "It's hugely popular, and the Anchorage cousins work with Caitlin to lure the tourists over to Roundhouse."

"But of course." Venus smiled at Walter. "That's how it has to be in business nowadays."

Recalling then that the biggest loss to the place was the shipping cargo outlet, Venus asked a question he already knew the answer to in order to keep Walter talking. Where was the cargo going instead, and how much did that affect the shipping companies?

Venus's instinct told him that Walter was not a viable suspect, and he was, in a way, relieved. After all, part two of his mission was to get Walter sobered up and back to work. Otherwise his retirement plans went out of the window, and that was the last thing that Venus wanted!

However, Venus had to wonder if Walter was drinking as much as people had been led to believe; he seemed perfectly compos mentis, and there was no telltale whiff of alcohol on his breath. He had walked with a steady stride as they skirted the harbour with its cobblestone quayside, passed the small slope to the beach area on the opposite side of the docking area and into the part where the new buildings of the Inn, Cafe and Shop were. Even if he hadn't researched Harbourtown Island, it was obvious the premises were new.

Again, time would tell what was the truth and what was fabrication of wild imaginations.

Chapter 34

Marissa blew her whistle and waved her arms at the swimmer who had gone beyond the safety boundaries of the red and yellow flags mounted in the sand to attract his attention.

"Swim between the red and yellow flags please!" She called out.

Different activities had different parts of the sea earmarked for them for the safety of the people involved in that particular activity. Red and yellow flags show which area of the beach is being patrolled by the lifeguards.

This area is safe for swimming, bodyboarding and the use of inflatables. Whereas, black and white chequered flags indicate a surfing area - designated for using surfboards and to keep these away from other bathers and water users.

Most people paid attention to where they were supposed to be, knowing that many of the dangers weren't apparent to the untrained eye. Again, most people knew to swim only at beaches that had lifeguards on patrol and not if any red flags warning of dangerous water conditions were present. Even then, those that did stray from the earmarked areas were soon apologetic and moved fast without any harm done.

Most of the beach incidents were basic mistakes by the beachgoers - be it sprained ankles from going into a hole in the sand, or a jellyfish sting, or sunburn from not wearing adequate protection. The trio were proud of the outstanding record on Bountiful Bay beach they maintained, and worked diligently to keep their hard won reputation.

Until the drifting boat incident when Nolan had been unwell, they hadn't needed to rescue anyone in the last 17 months. It was hoped by everyone that it would be at least that time frame again before their next casualty.

A hardstanding to one side of the beach had been set up with tables and chairs this summer. While plans hadn't yet come to fruition about what services to provide - perhaps a small shop selling beach essentials and food and drinks - some of artists and photographers had set out to capture the beauty of the area, keen to put their new skills learnt on Roundhouse to the test. Could it be another outlet for the Roundhouse cousins, Marissa wondered.

Walter set up interviews with everyone concerned. Firstly the villagers would be brought to the office singularly, then the lifeguards and Quentin could be interviewed over in Bountiful Bay. The same went for the Anchorage cousins on Roundhouse, and anyone from Conning mainland the Inspector may want to talk with.
Venus nodded at Walter's planning.
"By then, I should have negotiated a gap in the harbourmaster's schedule." Walter added tentatively.
Venus scoffed. "Nothing takes precedence over a murder inquiry, especially an empty harbour!"
From the way Walter flinched, it was obvious that the harbourmaster would not share this point of view, Venus noted. He wondered what he would encounter; bearing in mind then the Superintendent's description of the villagers - nitwits, misfits and eejits.
Readying himself before giving Walter the nod to begin, Venus wondered what was in store for him over the coming days... Such a long list could take days of interviews as opposed to hours. He sighed.

Hours in, and after an immeasurable amount of farcical ideas - the best of which Venus heard was of the killer using a frozen fish then disposing of it in the sea - many names had been scored off the potential suspects list. Venus had agreed to have Walter begin with those of little suspicion: those who had perfect alibis and could vouch for each other.

The four retired bachelors had been the worst for putting forward fanciful ideas.

Mr Mustard was an old fashioned gentleman who's strictness told of his previous life as an Army Colonel. His theory was that the killer had made a sharp getaway in his motorboat and would probably never be seen or heard of again.

Mr Boxer was a retired accountant with a taste for murder mystery books - a couch potato of sorts, as he had no interest in sports but instead he sat watching films and detective dramas, and read a lot. His ideas were very gory and involved ghosts.

Mr Plummer had run his own business, but as a carpenter not in the plumbing trade as his name dictated - much to Venus's amusement and surprise. Not blessed with much in the way of great imagination, his idea was that perhaps the victim had merely slipped and struck her head on something other than a cobblestone, as was the attending doctor's first thought.

Mr Halfpenny was a widower. He spoke highly of everyone on the island, and didn't have a bad word to say about anything. His theory was based on the frozen fish, although he didn't know why or how the murder was commited.

Sighing, Venus admitted the person gently knocking at the door, wondering who would be the next visitor. To his pleasure, it was the innkeeper's wife with a plate of food and a tankard of the local beer.

"Thank you, Tanya," Venus recalled at the last moment her

preference to be called by her christian name. "Alas, whilst on duty I cannot sample the local delights."

She produced a water pitcher and nodded. "I thought of that." She exchanged smiles with the Inspector. "Did you want to speak with me now?" Her voice was hesitant.

"If this is a convenient time for you, yes. Please sit down." Venus indicated the empty chair facing the desk, waiting until she sat down before beginning the new routine set of questions.

Learning that Tanya was the one responsible for bringing Ursula to Harbourtown, he detected she felt a little to blame for the death of the young lady everyone spoke so highly of. Next, asking her opinion of Shona and the relationship between the step-sisters, Venus had already suspected what she was going to say.

Shona had taken Ursula in when the rest of the family had turned their backs on her. The smaller shop premises in Conning made life together uncomfortable for them both, and the solution of Ursula running the shop here was a perfect one for all concerned. Shona didn't need to kill off her step-sister as she had, in effect, already got rid of her. That blew the theory of it being a family related motive.

Venus was however very interested to hear her thoughts on Roger's death; she - and many others - found it strange why a seasoned veteran would be out in his boat in such a storm? He had questioned the bachelors as to what their theories were - he was quite sure that none of them were involved, so it was agreeable to be more lax with their interviews.

Thanking her for her time, and again for the provisions she had brought, Venus smiled at her and was left in peace to think over the conversation.

Not only was Inspector Venus given free use of the office whilst the investigation took place, but one of the rooms for him also. Venus had been surprised to learn that there were two rooms for guests overnighting at the Inn, not entirely sure there was any call for it.

During their interview, David informed him of Walter's plight. Since things had turned so utterly terrible here, Walter had taken refuge in one of the rooms; drowning his sorrows and pints later, crawling upstairs to sleep it off until the next morning. Abandoning his home on the mainland, it was strange that he would rather sleep in a strange bed than his own.

That was one of Venus's pet hates of working away from home, so why would Walter deliberately choose to do so? Venus wondered if this was perhaps some kind of escape from the hell Walter thought his life had become - or was the poor man trying to chase ghosts by staying in Harbourtown where he'd lost first Roger, then Ursula?

Either way, it was his job to rescue Walter from the despair drowning him. Venus sighed again.

From the interviews he had already conducted, everyone spoke of Walter as a strong, dependable man. They all felt deeply sorry for him - for the loss of his best friend Roger and, by all accounts, a young lady who was special to him. Secondary was the burden he now had of the Commissioner breathing down his neck to quickly solve the murder for the good of the area.

Although he hadn't been privy to the conversation Walter would have had with the Commissioner, Venus could guess that it wouldn't have been an agreeable one. He too felt sorry for his comrade.

David confessed that as innkeeper, he was trusted with a

lot of secrets from his regulars. Venus's eyebrows raised in interest. That was something he'd heard of happening, but never actually encountered. It wouldn't happen in the big city, but somewhere with as cosy an atmosphere as mainland Conning or Harbourtown, he could imagine it occuring. Sadly, the titbits and gossip David had picked up was of no use to the investigation, but it gave Venus pause for thought.

Someone, somewhere, knew something and it was up to him to sniff it out.

At that point, the cat walked in. He pushed open the door and sauntered across the room as if he owned the place.

"Ah! I'm sure you've heard about Vimto, he's become a bit of a minor celebrity." David grinned.

Vimto stopped in mid stride upon hearing his name.

"I have, but I have not yet had the pleasure of meeting you." Looking at the cat, Venus found his gaze held.

Vimto stared him out until taking several steps forward to leap deftly onto the table between the two men. Automatically Venus offered one hand to let him sniff before stroking him. Curiously sniffing the pro-offered hand while maintaining eye contact, Vimto rubbed himself against the stranger's palm. This indicated instant acceptance in the animal/human world.

"Well Vimto, someone must know what happened." Venus mused, talking more to himself than anything else.

"Meow." The cat moved so that he sat right in front of the Inspector.

David was looking between them both, unsure of what to say.

"I'm here to find out the truth." Venus told him.

Vimto regarded him with a solemn look, almost as if to say 'yes, we need you to.'

"Do you know who did it?" He jokingly asked.

As David laughed, Vimto meowed. "Treating him like the cat equivalent of Lassie?" He got to his feet, shaking his head. "He'd be no use thinking clearly, he drinks beer." He joked again.

Vimto looked at him, eyes narrowed, as he followed David with his gaze from the room. Regarding Venus momentarily, he then jumped down from the table and disappeared out of the door; leaving the Inspector wondering if the animal was trying to communicate something to him.

Chapter 35

Yves had informed Venus while they talked of the differences between the lifeboat team and the lifeguards - Venus had assumed they were the same organisation, and they were. He told of each person's responsibility regarding the lifeboat, and was impressed that the Inspector already knew. However, Venus didn't know the general stats.

"RNLI lifeguards patrol over 240 beaches across the UK and the Channel Islands. They are qualified in lifesaving and casualty care, highly trained, strong and fit. They must be able to swim 200m in under 3½ minutes, and run 200m on sand in under 40 seconds. However, a good lifeguard rarely gets wet - 95% of a lifeguard's work is preventative."

Venus nodded, impressed by what he heard. Even if he hadn't known Yves delivered regular RNLI lectures, he would know it by the way the man was now talking.

"All RNLI lifeguards are equipped not only with the best training but the best equipment, so that they are able to deal with any situation. This includes: inshore rescue boat (IRB), rescue watercraft (RWC), patrol vehicle, all-terrain vehicle (quad bike), rescue board, rescue tube, VHF radio, binoculars, first aid responder bag, defibrillator.

Induction training for every lifeguard covers several key areas, providing them with the information they need to carry out their work safely and effectively. Knowledge is turned into practice during a series of staged scenarios, so that they are ready to hit the ground running on the first day of the lifeguard season.

The first key area is Casualty Care for Lifeguards (CC4LG) which is taught in situ on the beach. The course covers injury, illness and immersion, as well as triage for when casualties outnumber lifeguards. CC4LG also helps lifeguards gain confidence in using the equipment supplied at the lifeguard units.

Secondly, lifeguards are taught the safe use of an all-terrain vehicle (ATV), commonly known as a quad bike, including pre-operational safety checks, driving techniques, risk management and trailer usage. The ATV allows good manoeuvrability and all-round visibility, making it ideal for busy beaches.

Usually this is paired with the four-wheel drive (4WD) patrol truck. Used for patrolling, public safety announcements, launch and recovery, or simply as a base for lifeguards to work from at the water's edge. Through specialist training, lifeguards learn to drive this vehicle safely on the beach and in confined areas, recognise potential risks and hazards and learn how to recover the vehicle if it becomes stuck or 'bogged in'.

The fourth key piece of the lifeguarding kit is, of course, the Inshore rescue boat (IRBs). These give lifeguards the speed and manoeuvrability to get to the most hazardous of rescue scenes as quickly as possible. These are sturdy enough to operate in heavy surf conditions, yet light enough to be launched from the shore by two people. Every lifeguard is taught the skills and knowledge required to operate an IRB in surf conditions safely and effectively. Lastly, rescue watercraft - not to be confused with the IRBs." Yves paused to ensure the Inspector was still listening: when he nodded, Yves continued.

"Rescue watercraft (RWC) are fast and manoeuvrable in the hands of a well-trained operator, making them ideal in almost any condition. Especially capable of moving through very large surf and across big stretches of water quickly, they are normally operated by a single lifeguard.

But if an emergency arises, they can quickly pick up

another lifeguard from anywhere on the beach to help with complex rescues. They are equipped with a detachable foam rescue sled for ease of recovering and transporting casualties."

At this point, Venus wasn't sure if he was meant to applaud or not.

Yves asked a series of his own questions, and found that the Inspector could only give him basic answers - or rather, was only able to give him the basics. Offering his services whenever required, he left the office as bidden.

Vimto hobbled up the beach, unable to put much weight on his throbbing front left paw. The tide often washed up some interesting things, leaving them behind in the rock pools and parts of watery sand - he loved a good sniff around and maybe a dabble with his paw at seashells and seaweed. Some seaweed was tasty he had discovered quite by chance one day - every piece he tongue tasted to experiment with before beginning to chew, spitting out anything unpalatable.

Before today he hadn't encountered a live crab - he had seen plenty of them, mostly in skeleton parts, dotted around the shoreline. He liked to sniff and lick their shells, and did so this morning - only it was still alive and had been annoyed by the encounter, swiping at him with a claw before he could jump back. He yelped and snarled, but the crab had a strong hold on his paw and was not inclined to let go easily.

Shaking it off and trying to bite at it, eventually the angry crab released him: Vimto turned and ran like his life depended on it. Well, as much as he could with a very sore paw.

"Vimto!" Caitlin was the first one to see him and went

straight over, kneeling in the sand beside him as he sat with that paw hovered in the air.

"Meow!" He protested.

"What's wrong with your poor paw?" She reached towards him, but he backed off a hobbled few paces. "Let me see, I won't hurt you." She encouraged him.

"Me-ow," he lamented.

"Come here," she shuffled closer and grabbed him around the middle, bundling him into her chest.

"Caitlin?" Kim's voice carried across the water to her. "Is everything okay?"

"It's Vimto. His paw is bleeding."

Kim's eyebrows raised. "Vimto?"

"The lighthouse cat, the kids called him that and it's kind of stuck now." She explained. "He's not really Oxander's cat, he's a stray, but we all know him."

Kim had walked closer to them as she was talking and now could see the mixed ginger, white, black and brown animal tucked into her jacket. His paw hung limply from her arm and there was a fair amount of blood running from it.

"I've seen him before - didn't know his name." He chuckled. "Owch, that looks sore." Gently he stroked Vimto's head, talking soothingly to him. "What have you done?" He shook his head. "We have Quentin to sort us humans out, I wonder if we need to get you to a vet."

Vimto gave him a pitiful beseeching expression.

"There might be something in it, maybe it's a cut from glass or..." Caitlin trailed off. "We do need to get him seen. There's a new lady on Conning who is said to be a brilliant vet. I wonder if she can see him."

Kim nodded. "Beth Herd, she has a sterling reputation." He stroked Vimto's head again. "Poor boy; yes, Beth will sort you out. Do you want me to take you over there?"

They could both hear the hovercraft was returning at that moment. Caitlin shook her head. "Thanks, but we'll take him. Yves will drop me off."

"I'll call ahead and let her know you're on the way." Kim nodded. "Do you know where you're going? The veterinary practice is by the Medical Centre."

Caitlin smiled at him. "Thank you. We'll find it. C'mon Vimto, let's see Beth and get your poor paw sorted."

Striding towards her partner and his hovercraft, she couldn't wave to him or flag him down - but Kim did. He explained to Yves what the plan was while Caitlin got in and sat down with Vimto securely held against her chest. Yves nodded and quickly turned around, soon making the short trip back to the mainland with their precious cargo.

She wasn't sure how he would react to being in the hovercraft, but Vimto didn't complain or move. He was in too much pain, she supposed, and he had put his trust in her to help him.

"You poor thing." She whispered. "We'll get you better, boy." Dropping a kiss on the top of his head, his hair tickled her nose and cheeks. He was so soft and warm cuddled into her, and amazingly well behaved.

She had had nightmare visions of him trying to jump off her lap, and off the hovercraft, wondering how on earth she would catch him again - but he was no trouble at all.

Chapter 36

The interviewees Venus had instructed to be kept until last were in all probability the most meaningful, Walter had to agree. As he had earlier declared, it was doubtful they'd find a villain amongst the Treduggans, or the Bountiful Bay lifeguards or the Anchorages, Venus agreed.

He had more interest in the young fisherman. Firstly as the ex-boyfriend of the deceased; secondly, and perhaps more importantly, as the comrade of Roger and potentially a link to his suspicious death. If indeed there was a link of the two deaths, then the clue would lie with Nolan. Excitement coursed through Venus as he contemplated the idea of solving a double murder.

He summoned Nolan first.

Nolan began by explaining that Roger had chosen him to be his co-worker from the mainland some six months previously when trade was expected to double at Harbourtown. Roger had been a great influence on the young man, treating him almost like a son - Nolan recounted with tears in his eyes. His death had been a terrible shock to everyone - not only Harbourtown residents.

That was when Venus stopped him. "You knew he was out in his boat."

Nolan's eyes widened. "No, I didn't. Nobody knew."

Venus shook his head. "You were overheard whilst at the Inn saying you expected to find him there as he was doing something to his boat not long before."

"That is true." Nolan squirmed uncomfortably in his seat. "I wish I'd known what he was doing, I would have helped him. We might have saved him."

Venus gave a harrumph.

"Truly, I would have. He gave me a better life here." Nolan pressed.

"And Ursula, you two were an item not long before her death. What do you have to say about that then?"

Again his eyes widened. "You're very well informed."

"It is part of the job." Venus gave him a smile.

"Ursula and me, well, I." He corrected himself. "We only had a casual fling, it was nothing serious. She helped me to get over Roger's death and move on. She also helped look after me when I was ill. After I was rescued from the seagoing current."

Venus's eyebrows raised. "When was this?"

And so, Nolan told the tale of his collapse on board his boat one morning and how he'd been saved only by Marissa spotting his drifting boat as the sea tide took hold.

Venus nodded but said nothing, allowing the young man to rabbit on for a while longer about how he was saved from certain death; how grateful he was for Quentin's help and the lifeguards; how the work of the RNLI was so important. Earlier, Venus had virtually the same conversation with Yves, the ferryman. His had been a long interview, but an interesting one.

"This was the reason, you suppose, why the harbourmaster fought with you that day on the quayside?"

Nolan gasped. "You know about that too?"

"As I said, it's my job to know everything. Do continue."

Nolan looked very uncomfortable now, leading Venus to wonder what was coming. Again, he shifted in the chair. "I'd just docked in the usual place after a morning of being out fishing and selling when Oxander came bearing down on me. He wanted to talk about my relationship with her, called us both all sorts of names and refused to apologise.

Apparently he'd just been at the shop," he gestured over his shoulder as if he could point to it, "and café and caused a scene there. He was jealous of anyone getting attention from Ursula, as if he wanted her for himself."

Venus froze. Jealousy was a common motive and a common murderer came in the form of a jealous partner - was this the key to the investigation? He hardly dared hope!

"Did I say something wrong?" Nolan asked worriedly, interrupting Venus's thoughts.

"Not at all. Do continue." Venus waved him on, thankful that he'd kept the harbourmaster's interview for later.

Nolan continued to tell the tale, shuddering as he told how close he'd come to hitting his head on the harbour wall as he'd plummeted into the water by Oxander's hands. Yves coming to his rescue quickly and the crowd gathered around him full of sympathy was where the tale ended.

Venus knew this to be true as Yves himself had told exactly the same tale in exactly the same way. It was perhaps the truth that Nolan had nothing to do with either murder; and therefore it could also be true that neither death was connected.

"He didn't make any more trouble for you after that?" Venus asked.

Nolan shook his head. "Thankfully not." His face darkened. "Now everything has changed." Shaking his head sorrowfully, the earlier tears in his eyes returned. "I don't know if I want to stay here now or not." He almost whispered the last sentence.

Venus understood his emotions. Accepting that his earlier thought of the young man in front of him being potentially the guilty party had now sunk, he sighed deeply. Thanking him for his time, he sent Nolan home. He was puzzled, or so his expression spoke for him, but he left without question.

Chapter 37

Quentin had a busy morning of surgery appointments at Conning Medical Centre lined up. He was fortunate to be a part of a medical team - a dentist, a doctor and a nurse with one receptionist to arrange the necessary - so when he was required to up and leave for an emergency, no patients were effectively abandoned. Many times he had joked that they needed an animal service also at the centre: this week, his teasing was coming into fruition with the arrival of Beth and her exceptional veterinary skills.

Glancing up, out of the window, he saw a familiar figure hurrying up to the centre, looking a bit lost. Her expression and tense posture caused him to get to his feet and hurry out to her.

"Caitlin, what's wrong?"

"It's Vimto, he's hurt his paw, poor thing." She turned to show Quentin the injured paw. "I saw him on the beach as he usually does, having a sniff around, then I heard a yelp. I think something attacked him." She grimaced. "He was limping badly but trying to run away."

"Aww." Quentin looked at him sympathetically. "Well, we have just the person here today, Vimto. Beth will look after you and then Caitlin can take you home again."

Caitlin seemed a little more relaxed now that she'd spoken to him, and Vimto did also. The humans were looking after him, he had been right to trust them. They followed Quentin through the building, finding Beth waiting, having prepared for their imminent arrival after receiving Kim's call.

The Treduggan family would pay the necessary bill, Kim had told her before he had hung up, and he would call in the morning to find out what she had needed to do. She was under instructions to do whatever was necessary for the animal, no matter the cost.

Most people wouldn't do that for an animal that wasn't their own, and she was impressed. Even Caitlin and Yves taking the time out of their busy schedules to get him help was unusual. But she was about to learn that her new visitor was a very unusual cat...

"Hi," she smiled at Caitlin and Quentin. "This must be Vimto, please come straight through." She patted the high bench. "Put him down here please. Let's have a look at your poor paw, oh my, what a beautiful boy!" She gasped as his colouring was revealed when Caitlin stepped back from the bench where she had rested him. Initially, she had thought that he was a calico cat, only the ginger, white and black on display. "You are just gorgeous! No wonder everyone talks about you." She was talking to him softly and stroking him as he allowed her to get in closer.

He hissed as she almost touched his bad paw.

"Don't worry Vimto, I'm not going to hurt you on purpose, but I need to see what we're dealing with here." She shook her head. "That's a big cut. What did you do?"

Caitlin had given Quentin a quiet nod and he'd slipped out of the room moments earlier. She was reassured by Beth's manner immediately and knew Vimto was in very good hands. Putting a piece of gauze under his oozing paw, Beth very carefully picked up his sore leg without disturbing the actual cut. But that was enough - Vimto wailed.

"I'm sorry sweetheart, I know that hurts." Frowning, she peered closer. "It is a deep cut, no wonder he's in pain. It will need stitching." She said to Caitlin. "I will give him a small sedative to help, and after a rest here tonight, you can take him home."

"You want to keep him here?" Caitlin's eyes bulged.

165

Beth nodded. "I need to monitor him for infection. We don't want it to get worse." She gave her a kind smile. "You did exactly the right thing coming to me."

"Thank you, Beth." Caitlin's relief was a rushed sigh. "I hope he'll be okay."

"He'll be fine. Thanks to you. Don't let us keep you any longer, there must be a tour group waiting for you and Yves."

"Not yet but soon, you are right." She nodded, consulting her watch. "Thank you again. I'll call later to see how he is."

"Great." Beth nodded, turning her attention back to Vimto. "Let's wash this paw first, boy." She began.

It was Shona's turn to be interviewed next. Walter brought her to the office, leaving her with the Inspector alone as standard practice.

"Is it true that you wanted to get rid of your step-sister?" Venus began, speaking after consulting his notes.

"What?!" Shona's gasp was horrified.

"Did you, or did you not, thank Tanya for giving Ursula the job here and, I quote, 'getting her out of the way'?"

Shona seemed to consider her answer before she spoke. "She was under my feet, yes. She did have a tendency to push my buttons and took satisfaction in doing so, yes. But I would never cause her harm, no."

Venus shook his head. "Yours is a strong motive, even you must admit. Her sudden arrival here must have ruined your life."

"It did." Shona shrugged. "And then, it didn't. Things worked out, as they tend to do, and Ursula loved living here. She had her life and I had my own back again."

Changing tactics, Venus threw her a curveball. "Are you surprised she was murdered?"

"Of course I was!" Shona was on her feet now, leaning over the desk towards him. "How can you ask me that?! If I'd known she was in danger, I'd have protected her." A change came over her and she sat down again, her temper suddenly subdued.

Eyebrows raised at what he'd witnessed, Venus wondered if there was more to this than he had first thought. It was time to show his hand.

"You've come into a rather tidy inheritance now that she has gone."

Her expression was one of surprise. "How did you know that?"

Venus gave her a cunning smile, but didn't reply.

Shaking herself, Shona answered the question. "An inheritance of which was Ursula's, not rightfully mine." She looked the Inspector directly in the eye as she spoke. "You'll find that I have put plans in place to benefit the community with the money. I don't intend to make any personal gains from it."

"That is something else that I had learned." Venus told her.

"Good." Shona nodded, beginning to relax now. "I know Ursula could turn anyone against anyone else, she had that special knack," she grimaced, "but she wasn't the bad sort. Certainly not one who would be murdered to keep her mouth shut." She seemed to think for a moment. "I'm sorry I got angry. You are only doing your job. It can't be easy to ask all the questions and make sense of the puzzle."

Giving her a nod of acceptance of her apology, the nod was also to the fact that what she had stated was true - being the outsider in a case like this was notoriously difficult. Venus allowed a silence to fall between them before asking another question.

"Is that your opinion on the murder? That it was done to

keep her quiet?" He drew the conversation back to where they had left off.

Shona spread her hands wide. "I have no idea." She drew in a deep breath, slowly letting it go again. "Was it an accident? Was it deliberate? Was it a case of mistaken identity? Was it only meant to scare her off?" She shook her head. "I wish I knew. It's driving me crazy not knowing what happened to her - and why. She didn't deserve to die so young." Her voice tailed off as she began to cry.

This was why Venus had Walter hang on outside. How things were at the moment, they fulfilled the roles of good cop and bad cop - Walter being the local everyone knew and respected made Venus the bad one, but only by default.

Quentin looked at his phone as it rang, seeing a familiar number on the screen. He hoped this was not another emergency call over to Harbourtown, and answered it with his breath held.

"Good afternoon. I'm sorry to interrupt," Kim began, "can we ask you for a favour please?"

"Of course." Quentin nodded, glad that it wasn't another emergency and relaxing in that knowledge. "What do you need me to do?"

"At some point, could you nip round to the vets and pick up Vimto?" Kim smiled. "Caitlin is worried about him, but can't get over until tomorrow, despite Yves being over there within the next hour. The poor creature has already been in overnight. Don't worry about the bill, I've already settled it."

"Sure." Quentin agreed. "Is he ready now?"

"Yes. Thank you. The sooner we get the pesky scamp back, the sooner things will settle over here." He laughed again. "Tanya wants to look after him at the Inn until his paw heals properly, and I agree. It's probably best that he's out of Oxander's way also."

"How on earth are you going to keep him indoors?" Quentin asked.

"We'll shut him in a room for a few days and keep feeding him. That ought to do it." He paused. "It was Beth's idea, and I trust that she knows best."

Quentin nodded, smiling with a sudden thought. "Does he have the cone of shame on?" He joked.

"I don't know." Kim admitted. "He might just have a bandage."

"I'd best go prepared." Quentin mused. "Every patient needs some kind of blackmail to do something for their own good." He joked.

"Good luck!" Kim laughed. "You don't need to come all the way out here, just hand him over to Yves."

"That'll be like passing the parcel, poor Vimto!" Quentin laughed.

They ended the call. Quentin checked his schedule, double checking it was as he thought - one patient to see before he could spare the time to go on his special errand.

Vimto was getting VIP treatment, or should that be VIC - Very Important Cat - treatment? Shaking his head, Quentin smiled at the thought that Vimto must be the most spoiled stray ever.

Yves discovered Vimto was in a borrowed cat carrier from Beth's veterinary practice. Although Yves was sure that he wouldn't have tried to escape once on the hovercraft, he kept him in there. Historically speaking, the cat had been used to travelling. When you are out of sorts as Vimto would no doubt be because of his trauma, he might be less cautious than usual.

It was best not to risk such precious cargo, knowing there would be several members of Harbourtown who would never forgive him if something happened to Vimto whilst supposedly in his care.

Quentin waved them off, and Vimto meowed his farewell happily enough, almost as if the doctor had been talking solely to him! Yves smiled at the thought. Upon their arrival, Yves knew to take Vimto to the Inn where Tanya had made preparations for his stay while his paw healed. On his next return to Conning, he would have time to moor the craft and return the carrier to Beth.

Vimto watched through the gate on the carrier as Yves took him off the hovercraft, up the quay and across the harbour to the Inn. Tanya had food and water waiting, Vimto saw, and had created him a fleece lined cushioned bed. She smiled when Yves exclaimed that this was the Ritz for cats.

Tentatively, Vimto hobbled out of the carrier, sniffing around the room. They both watched him for a few minutes before leaving, ensuring the door was closed securely behind them.

Vimto was curled up asleep in his new bed when Tanya checked on him half an hour later: he hadn't eaten yet, but he had taken a drink before settling down. Another hour later, he was at the double bowl, eating and drinking noisily.

She came into the room then; he looked up at her and gave a strange meow-purr. Squatting down beside him to stroke him, she told him that she'd be looking after him for a while and he was to be given free run of the Inn once his paw had healed - but there was to be no drinking the local brew.

In return, he gave her a look as if to deny all notion of what she was referring to. But they all recalled his antics after trying some of the local beer - it had taken weeks for

170

David to stop complaining about the cat's wind issues after the alcohol!

"You might find some spiders around." She added. "You can have as many of those as you can catch. But don't bring them to me, okay?" She shuddered with the thought.

He regarded her, tilting his head sideways.

"Oxander told us that you sorted out the rat problem at the lighthouse; well, there are no rats here. Your diet will improve." She joked.

"Meow!" His eyes lit up at that.

"We'd better not spoil you too much or you won't want to go back to the lighthouse." She joked.

He regarded her again, but silently - as if to say, I'll be the judge of that! Then, she could have sworn, he winked at her. Did cats wink?!

Chapter 38

"Dr Farma, I have no doubt that you have your own suspicions about the murderer." Venus began the second Quentin sat down in the office opposite him.

Quentin's mouth fell open.

"In your profession, you see people from all walks of life. That will make you a good judge of character."

Quentin remembered himself and closed his mouth. "That is a very shrewd observation." He sat back in the chair; a hint of a smile danced on his lips.

"A truthful one, would you say?"

He nodded. "I also judge people by how they treat animals."

It was interesting to hear him say that, especially so soon into the interview. Venus nodded.

"How do you view the residents of Harbourtown?" Venus dived straight in. He almost smiled when he recalled the Superintendent's phrase.

"As a whole, they are friendly and helpful. That has aided the popularity of the tours and the island's overall revenue."

Venus nodded again. "You are seemingly the only man who didn't have a fling with Ursula."

Quentin smiled at that statement. "I may have done, had I not sworn off women before I arrived here." He pulled a face.

Venus wondered if he would add to that statement without prodding. Also he wondered if the doctor needed prodding - was that entirely relevant to the investigation? Venus decided it wasn't. Recalling the description of the villagers from the Superintendent, he inserted this into their conversation.

"A bunch of nitwits, misfits and eejits was the collective term I was given for the Harbourtown villagers. I think that is scathing and untrue considering the people I have met so far." Venus gave him a smile, receiving one in reply.

"I'm inclined to agree with you on that. However, every place has its own misfits and nitwits." He almost laughed saying the terms.

Now he was relaxed, Venus knew it was the best time to turn to the serious questions. "Are you surprised to find that the harbourmaster is a danger not only to himself but to others?"

Quentin drew in a deep breath slowly. "Oxander is undoubtedly very good at his job."

"But?" Venus prompted.

"But I have to admit that you are right to say that he is a danger." His gaze went out of the room and into his thoughts. "I did wonder if it was some sort of reaction, at first."

It was Venus's turn to be confused. "Reaction to what?"

"Upon his return from the accident, he was still on an amount of medication - painkillers and muscle relaxants mostly." Quentin sighed heavily. "Stress, strain and the limitations of pain can be a toxic mixture. I advised him that it was too soon to return, but he would have none of it."

This did sound like the character Venus was building a good picture of.

Nodding, Venus ensured he correctly noted the details before continuing with the questioning. "What does your intuition tell you about the young fisherman, Nolan?"

"Nolan is a bright young man who works hard for what he wants and isn't afraid to settle for a simpler life. He is wise beyond his years." Quentin saw Venus's surprised expression and added: "in my opinion."

Venus changed tact, sensing an opportunity to confirm an important thought. "Do you find the local policeman

173

lacking?"

"Lacking?" he repeated, his expression confused at the use of the word. "Walter is methodical, certainly. He does seem to keep the peace in the area, to be fair."

Venus snorted. "You are forgetting the arsonist who burnt half of Conning to the ground and would have gotten away with it if it had been left to Walter's detecting work."

"Ah but it wasn't." Quentin leant back in the chair, somewhat relaxed now.

"Thank goodness it wasn't or there may have been who knows what sort of trouble." Venus corrected.

The two men eyed each other for a short while until the interview continued, and then concluded. Venus had a lot to think about.

Shona twisted her hair nervously as she awaited Vicar McClulland. She was glad of the distraction of customers coming into the shop, even if they didn't intend to buy - something that usually irritated her, unless she too wanted to talk to someone.

The Vicar was truly lovely: a man whom everyone felt comfortable with. He had made the whole awful thing so much more bearable, and although she supposed that was part of his job, she was beyond grateful. Thanks to the large amount of money that she had been sent by the family, the remaining balance on the new church roof would be found - she intended to give him the good news at their meeting.

Although she wasn't particularly religious, Shona understood why a lot of people were - having something solid to fall back on such as your faith was highly underrated in times of trouble. It was no wonder that many lost souls had found peace in the hands of God.

They exchanged pleasantries while Shona made them

both a cup of tea when Vicar McClulland arrived. Sitting down to business, Shona took a deep breath. All Creatures Great and Small, Abide by Me and The Lord's Prayer were standard hymns. Good, that was fine. Something unusual that was likely to cause a ruckus was not what she wanted.

The church could have fresh flowers on the day - some late blooming roses perhaps? Shona nodded with the idea, thinking it sounded lovely. The graveyard on the hill overlooking Conning had the sun every afternoon, would a plot there for the burial be suitable, or was a more sheltered spot preferred? Shona nodded again, glad that no words were required as she couldn't think of what she could possibly say.

As they lapsed into silence, it was Shona's turn to talk. Not only did she have the money necessary, she also wanted to donate to the church roof fund. Adding that she hoped the amount would be sufficient to pay for the rest of the renovation costs, and showing him the amount she was poised to send, she saw his shock. But it was a pleasant shock.

He beamed and thanked her, double checking before he allowed her to electronically send the money across into the church bank account that she was sure of the decision. She assured him that yes she was sure, and they exchanged smiles.

Talking then about her plans for a lifeboat shop in the not too distant future, he waxed lyrical about the brilliance of the idea and the brave work undertaken by RNLI volunteers. Then, they were interrupted by the shop bell declaring the arrival of a customer, so Shona left him with his cup of tea to see to her customer's needs.

Upon her return, he promised not to take up any more of her time and bid her farewell, but not before checking on her welfare and reiterating the discussions they'd had last time - if she needed anything, or she simply wanted someone to talk to, she was only to say.

Humbled by the offer she smiled and thanked him, watching him leave. As last time, a huge burden felt lifted from her shoulders. She sighed deeply.

Despite his bandaged and obviously painful paw, Vimto could still get around. As a result of his new lodgings, it was easier for him to get into the public bar at the Inn where the regulars were now used to him. In fact, some of them actively looked for the unusually coloured cat.

"Here he is." The shout went up.

Venus looked up as Vimto came into the room properly, giving the sympathy limp as if his very life depended on it. Smiling before he returned to his thoughts, he watched for a moment as people rushed over to the cat: picking him up and hugging him; patting his head and telling him what a brave boy he was, and some such things.

Venus hadn't observed just how many people spoiled the cat - offering some of the nibbles, not daring to give him any of their drinks as David had a close eye on them, patting the seat beside them and lifting him up so he could perch there as the centre of attention. But Walter had.

"He likes everyone, and everyone likes him." He said, his voice soft. "It's like he's our mascot."

Nolan was next to lavish attention on Vimto, and Venus looked up, remembering what Quentin had said - you could judge a person's character by how they treated animals. Nolan was spoiling him as if the animal was his own. Truth be told, Venus was pleased to see it.

Oxander was at the bar, and walked across with his glass to sit not far from Nolan. Venus assumed that Vimto would go to him next - after all, they did share living accommodation. Tanya came across then, interrupting what might have naturally happened next between the man and the animal.

"I hope you don't mind," she said to Oxander, "all those steps are too hard for him at the moment with his bad paw. We'll look after him."

Oxander shrugged, his air one of nonchalance. "He's not my cat. I've said it before." His expression was neutral as he took a mouthful of his drink. "If you want to look after him, that's fine. You can't stop a cat doing something he doesn't want to do." He smiled at her, his gaze travelling over to Vimto.

Vimto was now standing on the empty chair beside Nolan, his gaze locked on Oxander. Tail swishing with annoyance, he growled.

"Vimto!" Tanya gasped.

Even Nolan looked shocked. "He didn't like you the last time he saw you." He said to Oxander. "What did you do to him?"

"I haven't done anything to him, for God's sake!" Oxander sighed exasperatedly. "Look. He's a cat. Animals are strange. And he's had a trauma, he's bound to be feeling out of sorts." He shrugged. "If you want to stay here, that's fine by me." He talked directly to Vimto. "Be nice for Tanya and David while they look after you."

Vimto hissed at him.

"That's happened before?" Venus asked Walter.

He nodded. "As Nolan said, last time we were all here, the cat was fine with everyone except Oxander. Weird huh?"

"Very." Venus frowned. The cat had been friendly and playful even with a complete stranger, so why would he turn against the person who kept him in food and shelter?

"That's animals for you." Walter shrugged. "Totally

unpredictable."

Shaking his head, Venus wasn't wholly convinced. Vimto had a grudge against his former friend, but why? It was an omen of some kind.

All Venus needed to do now was figure out what…

Chapter 39

At the lifeguard hut on Bountiful Bay beach, Venus sat surrounded by Will, Dwayde and Marissa, promising not to take up too much of their time. Rightly so, their attention was halved - although the trio were no longer technically on duty, they couldn't switch off their instincts whenever they were beachside.

Getting them to briefly tell what they knew about Harbourtown and its residents, Venus learned nothing new. Much as he had suspected, they all told the same story - this was why he'd broken protocol with a group interview instead of singular sessions.

They all praised the work of Oxander, and Yves and Quentin, professionally and personally when it came to RNLI matters. The mens' positions were explained, then Venus was given a rundown of how it worked in their community.

There was no reason to doubt the characters of Yves or in fact Quentin - and the lifeguards' story sealed the truth. It was just not possible that either of them would cause harm to human life, never mind someone as mild mannered and kind as Ursula. It had been a thought that most people had echoed; most people had no idea who could have done such a thing; but the truth remained that someone had, Venus reminded them.

Nolan too had become a vital member of the lifeboat crew from Harbourtown, having been involved with the Conning crew before his move across to the island. The necessary training to have him upskilled hadn't involved too much effort on anyone's part - another feather in Nolan's cap. His brief relationship with Ursula was deemed a healthy and honest one - he too was not likely to have killed her, be it in a fit of passion or otherwise.

They then asked if the Inspector believed Ursula's death had not been an accident. Choosing to inform them that the angle of the blow meant that it was by no means caused accidentally, Venus saw them all pale. It was obvious until then none of them had placed truth in the news that it had been a murder.

Before leaving, Venus questioned them on the incident of Roger's death. They also didn't understand why Roger had been out in the storm, but maintained that his death was caused by natural causes. This was obvious because of the dangers of being in a boat in open water during a thunderstorm.

Thanking them for their time and apologising for dragging them into the investigation, none of the trio protested, Venus noted. It seemed that despite Venus thinking there was a link between the deaths, there perhaps really wasn't one. He couldn't help feeling a little subdued.

The interview with Caitlin also was standard. Venus was not surprised to hear nothing new.

He threw her a curveball. "What did you make of Ursula's relationships with Nolan and Oxander?"

"I wasn't concerned about her being with Nolan at all. They are, were," she corrected herself, "the same age and got on well together. With Oxander, it was different." She sighed. "I did worry about Oxander's mental stability after the incident with Nolan on the quay."

Venus nodded. "You won't be surprised to know that you haven't been the only one to say that."

Caitlin shook her head. "I went to Ursula to warn her that Oxander was a danger. She laughed it off and said that I was just being paranoid."

Venus looked at her intently. "You suspected he would harm her?"

Caitlin shrugged. "I wasn't sure what to expect. I didn't know where his mind was. He usually doesn't have a bad word to say about anyone, but he tore into Ursula at the shop, and then not long later, Nolan." She shook her head. "Apparently when Kim went to speak to him, they argued. Nobody has ever argued with Kim, and Oxander is usually so calm and in control. It was frightening."

Venus mused over this information for a while. "You wouldn't have put it past him to have argued with Ursula again?"

"I don't know what happened." Caitlin was quick to say. "I'm not pinning the blame on him, but..." Her voice trailed off. "Maybe it was to do with his accident, you know, he took a bad bang on the head."

"When was this?" Venus frowned. "The same time he had the accident at the lighthouse?"

"Yes." She nodded. "By all accounts, it wasn't only because he had something broken in his leg that they had to use the rescue helicopter."

Venus's eyebrows raised.

"Quentin will know more. He was with him." She added.

"Dr Farma also supervised his care, did he not?" Venus checked.

"I get the feeling I have said too much." She almost whispered, her cheeks colouring with embarrassment.

"Not at all," Venus reassured her. "I need to know everything, so every detail you can think of is important to me. Can you think of anything else?"

As it was, she couldn't. But that didn't matter. Venus had an important lead to follow up.

Chapter 40

Whilst Walter took Venus across the harbour to his boat for the excursion across to Roundhouse, they passed the lighthouse. Pointing out to the Inspector that Felix was the name of the lighthouse, Oxander appeared at the bottom of the lighthouse steps before either policeman could speak. He needed no introduction, it was obvious who he was - and Venus was keen to test him out.

Venus smiled, nodding at the 17th century lighthouse. "Lots of people must assume that Felix is the cat."

It was actually in very good condition for its age, despite the treatment it must have endured over centuries of rough weather. That in itself opened up suspicion in Venus's mind.

Oxander and Walter both looked at him in surprise.

"Well, it is a common cat name, thanks to the popular cat food adverts." Venus continued.

Oxander gave Walter a look as if to say who is this nutcase? Venus wondered if Oxander had thought the Inspector was perhaps not looking at him when he did it, for when their eyes met, Oxander's gaze turned away hastily.

If he hadn't already had the lowdown on him, Venus would have immediately been alerted by Oxander's unusual careless attitude in front of a police Inspector, especially one investigating a murder in the area.

"Should I be aware of anything before we go in?" Venus asked.

"Go in?" Oxander questioned, his eyes wide in horror. "Go in where?"

"The lighthouse." Venus clarified, giving him a stern look.

Shaking his head, Oxander tried to dissuade his visitor. "There's nothing to see. A great view of the harbour, most of the village and the sea, certainly. But that's it." Shuffling his feet nervously, his gaze fell to the cobbles.

"Not even I've been up there." Walter gestured to the very top of the lighthouse where the beacon was. The observation deck was around it and Venus could imagine there wasn't a lot of room up there. "Too many bloody steps. I don't know how you do it." He turned to Oxander. "Probably because you are young and fit." He answered his own question.

As Venus cleared his throat meaningfully, Walter seemed to check himself.

"We are off to Roundhouse but when we return, the Inspector wants to have a word with you at my office. Be ready."

Oxander's mouth gaped open, but before he could challenge the idea, the two policemen took their leave.

Quite convinced that the culprit was from Harbourtown, nonetheless in the interest of fairness, Venus knew he had to interview the people in the surrounding areas.

He wondered how the villagers were looked upon by their neighbours. By all accounts, the Anchorage cousins had their hands full with their business on the island, and as a result didn't have many dealings with the comings and goings on Harbourtown or Conning mainland. By having their own boat to fetch supplies and students, they were in effect self-sufficient.

Walter and Venus were given a friendly welcome by the oldest cousin, Faith. She was the manager and general organiser of the business, with Joy as the painter and Hope as the photographer. Faith was in her forties, Venus guessed, with her cousins in their early to mid thirties.

Taller but rounder, Faith had a natural gift for project

management - a born organiser, she excelled at any challenge. Joy looked artistic, petitely proportioned with dark curly hair and a loose outfit of clashing colours. Hope was more smartly dressed, and the only one with glasses.

Between them, they gave the Inspector a rundown of the schedule at Roundhouse - lessons in technique and observation, free time for sketching and painting, tripod and settings tutorials, colour visualisation... Venus had to admit most of it went over his head, as he was a writer but not actually that artistic. They ran an efficient business as you'd expect from three talented women, and were always looking for ideas for future opportunities.

None of them were on the island of Harbourtown during the storm. They had their own guests to attend to, and they were all able to vouch for each other - as Venus and Walter had suspected.

Venus didn't waste much more time on Roundhouse, knowing his attention could now turn to the harbourmaster.

"My condolences," Venus began.
Oxander's head shot up from the floor where his gaze had been for the last few minutes of silence. Deliberately Venus had kept him waiting to see how he would react. His expression was confused.
"Ursula was your beloved, was she not?" Venus elaborated.
He nodded. "We didn't have the best start, but... Yes." Oxander shrugged, as if to shrug off the memories.

The gesture reminded Venus of his aloofness at the Inn when Tanya had approached him about Vimto's welfare, and how that had seemed a strange attitude to have.
"Tell me about it." He prompted.
He frowned. "About what?"
"The start."

"Of what?" Oxander's frown deepened.

Venus sighed. So this was the game, was it? He too could play along. "Your relationship." He pressed. "Ursula had more than one lover on the island, I believe."

"Had being the operative word." Anger flashed in Oxander's dark eyes. "I made sure that we were one, not a party." He snorted.

"Yes, I have heard about that."

"What does that mean?" The reply was shot back instantly.

"It means, Mr Knowe," Venus began, "that your behaviour points to you as the most likely person to have murdered Ursula."

Oxander's face drained of colour. "What?!" He thundered. He seemed to gather himself the next moment. "Why would I? And, and," he stuttered, "how could I - everyone knows that my duty is to remain at the lighthouse during a storm. That's where I was, the whole time, you can ask anyone."

"Hmm," Venus mused, "the perfect so-called alibi."

"It is not so-called! It is true!" Oxander slammed his fists into the table and jumped to his feet, beginning to pace the small room.

"Just about everyone else has at least one witness stating where they were at the time of the murder." Venus consulted his notes, careful to speak calmly and slowly. "Most people were together at the Inn or at home. There are only a handful of you who were alone, and have nobody to vouch for your story."

Oxander's expression relaxed. "Everyone can see me from the lighthouse." He spoke almost gleefully, Venus noticed.

"Nobody would have been looking for you. Everyone knows to shelter away from windows during the most vicious storms." Venus pointed out.

"What are you insinuating?" Oxander leant over the table

menacingly.

"Mr Knowe, I am merely stating the facts as I come to them." Venus held his stony gaze; Oxander soon broke away.

His expression changed again and he turned away from the Inspector. "I loved her, I wouldn't have hurt her." He spoke after a while.

"Loved?" Venus pounced on the word. "You can still love someone when they are no longer living."

"What does that mean?" Oxander spat.

Venus shrugged. "It means what it does."

Huffing, Oxander stormed out of the building. From the slamming of doors, it sounded as if he'd huffed all the way out of the Inn.

Venus watched his progress with interest from the window of the small room - he went off in the direction of the harbour and sure enough up to the lighthouse, where he soon disappeared from view.

That had been the most interesting initial interview Venus had ever encountered.

Chapter 41

It struck him that he needed something with her writing so that he could copy it to make the note more genuine.

The place to find it would be the shop, or maybe the room above it where she stayed. But how would he get in?!

Access was via the Inn or the Café. There was no possible way he would be able to get through to the shop from the Inn, there was always someone around who would see and stop him, questioning his actions.

So that left the café. Somehow...

"Doctor, tell me about the accident that befell Mr Knowe." Venus began. "There is evidence that his judgement may have been affected by the accident."

Quentin frowned. "You mean his strange behaviour?" He fell silent. "I did wonder if it was caused by the blow to his head, but I insisted at the hospital that they perform a brain scan. Everything was clear. As my patient, I ensured he had the best treatment."

"I'm sure that you did." Venus spoke soothingly. "I'm not questioning your skills or patient care, I simply wonder if there was a chance that his character could have altered, temporarily or permanently."

"It is entirely possible." Quentin replied after a pause. "During his recovery at my home, I had the opportunity to monitor him regularly. He received many visitors and nothing untoward ever happened." He grimaced. "Initially, he and Ursula were at loggerheads, but that was soon resolved."

"They were?" Venus sat up straight in the chair. "Why did you not inform me of this before?"

"I didn't see the relevance." Quentin shrugged. "It was

natural for him to be annoyed with her - she caused his accident. But that's all it was - an accident. She apologised and he forgave her. Their friendship blossomed into as normal a romance as any other."

"You didn't consider him a danger to the young lady?"

"No." Quentin's frown deepened. "Absolutely not. They didn't argue after that. There was harmony, and things were going well."

"I am not so sure." Venus told him. "It sounds as if he could have murdered her. As yet, I don't know the reason or reasons, but he had opportunity and motive."

Quentin went white. He neither moved nor spoke for several minutes, so Venus decided a diversion was required.

Relocating into the fresh air would help him get over his shock, and allow the interview to continue. The feeling that he was getting somewhere was growing, in Venus's mind.

On their way outside, they met Tanya in the corridor.

"Quentin, whatever is the matter?" Tanya's voice rose in horror, seeing his pale face.

He couldn't answer.

Venus gave her a small smile. "Doctor Farma has had rather a shock." Gently he patted his shoulder. "We will be outside, could you please bring some of your strongest whisky? Neat."

Nodding with the instruction, she turned to the task in hand but watched as the two men vacated the premises.

Hurrying out to them within a few minutes, she also thought to take two glasses of water, which then necessitated a tray to balance them all on. Putting the tray down on the table, her attention returned to him.

"Quentin," she tried, touching his arm, "what is it?"

Still, he shook his head, unable to find his voice.

"You're shaking." Tanya put an arm around his shoulders

comfortingly. "What did you say to him?" She shot an accusing stare at Venus. "Quentin would never do anything to hurt anyone."

Venus was almost amused by her threat. "Believe me, I know he wouldn't." He spoke truthfully.

Quentin found his voice then. "It's not what you're thinking." He whispered.

"Oh." Tanya stopped. She seemed for a moment to not know what to do, or say. "Should I go?" She withdrew her comfort from him, looking between the two men.

He lapsed into silence again.

"Thank you for the drinks." Venus replied. "We'll let you know if we need anything else." He added, effectively dismissing her.

Still, she hesitated. "Will you be okay?" She asked Quentin. "I've never seen you like this."

Closing his eyes, he nodded. That did it; reluctantly Tanya left. Guilt threatening to strangle him, Quentin couldn't move even to take the drink in his hand and have a sip. He was still deathly white.

"Nobody can know what we have discussed." Venus began. "I need to have everything in place before I can work on a confession and an arrest."

He nodded. "Of course."

"Please do not think that this is in any way your fault." Leaning across the table, Venus touched his arm.

Quentin's head shot up so fast, Venus almost smiled. "How did..."

"It is human nature to think that such things would not have happened if we'd done this, or that, or the other. You are in the position of being plagued with guilt for no good reason for a lot of the time that you help people in your line of duty. I am the same." Venus explained. "Once the shock wears off, you will see that I am right."

He nodded, much to Venus's relief.

"I suggest that you cancel whatever plans you had next and take some time to regroup."

He nodded again, and Venus could see some colour returning to his cheeks.

"What in the name of hell is going on here!" David stormed across to where the two men were sitting in privacy at an outside table.

Venus was about to speak when Quentin cut him off.

"Nothing to worry about." He managed to flash David a smile. "I'm in shock, that's all."

David's demeanour changed instantly.

"No doubt Tanya told you her thoughts." He continued.

David nodded, and looking between the men, relaxed when he saw the situation himself. "I'm sorry to interrupt," he began, looking specifically at Venus.

He waved off the apology. "It is a refreshing change for me to see compassion." Giving them both a smile, Venus got to his feet. "I must meet with Walter. Take your time and heed what I said."

He told Quentin, getting him to nod before leaving him at the outside table, knowing that he would do as he was told. He was, after all, the sensible sort.

Chapter 42

As daft as it sounded, it wasn't real until they carried the coffin into the church. Watching as it passed the congregation before being laid gently to rest onto the plinth at the front of the pews, Shona couldn't get the thought out of her head that Ursula was trapped in there. She wanted to run over and tear into it to get her out. The truth hit her full on right there and then that she was never coming back - Ursula was gone forever.

Suddenly overwhelmed, Shona collapsed under the weight of her grief. As she was sitting at the very front, she sprawled onto the floor, face first.

None of her family or anyone from Ursula's side of the family were present at the funeral, so the church was filled with residents of Conning and Harbourtown. In a way, that was preferable to having anyone there who felt forced to attend. Tanya and David sat beside her, with Nolan, Quentin and Oxander in the adjacent row.

The vicar reached her first, not much before Quentin did. Profusely embarrassed, Shona insisted she was fine - she hadn't been unconscious long and she hadn't hit her head - and that they should continue as she didn't want to make a fuss.

She spent the rest of the service with her eyes closed, Tanya's arm linked through hers while her other arm was draped around her shoulders. David moved so that he now sat on Shona's opposite side, ready to catch her if she passed out again, keeping half an eye on her and half on the service.

A terrible thought crept over the crowd - was the murderer also here? It was more than likely. The vicar was doing an amazing job in what was a very difficult situation of leading the service and making it beautifully memorable; however, they couldn't get out of the church fast enough to Shona's mind.

At the Inn, where they held their second village wake, Isaac was holding the fort, allowing both parents to attend the service. Cecillia had free reign at The Empty Tankard on the mainland for the short time that everyone was away, but she was watched by a few staff members who had worked for David and Tanya for years.

Tanya then fussed over her friend's condition - bringing her a cold pack for her now swollen lip and mouth. Shona had everyone commiserating with her and trying to console her when really all she wanted to do was to hide away by herself for a while. It was all very touching, and she was amazed by the outpouring of love for her and Ursula - in all honesty, it was a bit too much for her to cope with.

She cried on Quentin's shoulder when he came to check on her, worried about her physical and emotional state. His concern tipped her over the edge of what she could cope with.

"I think we should take you home." Tanya spoke softly to her, looking at Quentin for his agreement. "It's been a very draining day. You did so well to arrange it all, and it was beautiful. Now you need some time to yourself."
Caitlin and Yves joined the three then. "I agree." They both spoke together, sharing a smile.

"I'll take you home whenever you want." Yves offered.

"That's okay, I'll take her." Quentin stepped in, much to the raised eyebrows of the room.

It didn't take much to get the rumour mill started up..

Kim shifted awkwardly in his seat. "My mother and father

192

send their apologies." He began. "Of course you are welcome to return to interview them separately if you deem it necessary."

Giving him the benefit of the doubt, Venus smiled. "I'm not sure at this stage yet, but thank you for the suggestion. I will let you know, in time." Pausing, Venus considered how to follow this opening. "I understand that you are responsible for the overall running of the island, is that correct?"

He nodded. "I represent the family's best interests, and those of the villagers."

"It must be a juggling act, at times."

Kim nodded. "Not much goes wrong, to be fair."

"That's down to your effective management." Venus nodded at him. Kim didn't respond. "How long have you been living on the island?"

"I was adopted by the Treduggan family at six years old. They've always been here, the place goes back generations."

"So...?"

"Sorry. So, I've been here almost thirty years now." Kim gave a relaxed smile. "It doesn't seem like that long sometimes."

"You never wanted to leave?"

He spread his hands wide. "Why should I want to be anywhere else? We have all we need here."

Venus gave him a genuine smile. "Some people spend their whole lives looking for the sort of harmony you have achieved here, and never find it."

"We are extremely lucky." Kim nodded. "But you're not here to talk about me. You want to know what I know about the murder."

Venus's eyes widened. "You know something about the murder?"

"I would say so." Kim nodded. "There were two figures on the quayside in that storm. Both in waterproofs head to toe so I couldn't see who it was."

"How did you manage to see through the rain?"

"I have a telescope for watching the ships on the horizon. I also keep an eye on the village." He shrugged. "Just to be nosey."

Venus laughed at his honesty. "I'm sure anyone would be the same in your position."

Kim nodded, his expression grateful. His annoyance rose to the surface. "This is the most dreadful thing! Murder! Such a waste of life."

Nodding in agreement, Venus wasn't surprised by Kim's annoyance. If his responsibility was the smooth running of Harbourtown, which it was, he would be feeling like he missed something somewhere and perhaps he might feel as if it was - to a degree - his fault.

Venus felt sorry for him. "You didn't know what would happen." He consoled him.

Wordlessly, Kim shook his head. "She was such a lovely girl."

Fighting the reaction to roll his eyes, Venus also withheld a sigh. It seemed that even Kim had fallen for Ursula's charms. No doubt the telescope aided him in keeping a watch on her... But perhaps innocently, Venus reminded himself not to jump to conclusions, especially as it was something he was prone to doing.

"Were you an item?" Venus began.

He shook his head. "She wouldn't have looked at me." He gave a sad smile.

"I don't see why not." Deciding to pander to his whims, Venus realised that he might glean more information from this conversation if he acted like he was on Kim's side. "You have everything going for you."

He shook his head. "She fell for Oxander, and after his accident," he laughed quietly, "ironically caused by her thoughtfulness, she became a Florence Nightingale to him." He sighed. "If you'll pardon the expression."

Venus's frown showed his confusion. "Oxander spent his respite period with Doctor Farma, at his home."

Kim nodded. "Yes, but he sent for her every day, and Quentin picked her up. I'm guessing he did it to keep the peace." He smiled a wicked smile. "Quentin is no pushover, but he knows how to get the best out of people."

"If they spent so much time together, and it seems everyone who saw Ursula fell under her spell, how come it didn't work on him?" Venus wondered aloud.

Kim shrugged. "Rumour has it that he has sworn off women. Bad news in his past, that sort of thing."

"Hmm." Venus began to wonder if Quentin did actually want to be a lover of Ursula's.

"I wouldn't doubt him." Kim continued quickly. "I never saw anything other than a common courtesy to her, as he displays to everyone else. Quentin is as reliable as the proverbial rock."

"He does strike me so." Inclining his head, Venus took in Kim's serious and solemn expression. "What do you think about Nolan?"

"Nolan and Ursula had a fling. I saw them out on his boat one evening." He smiled with the memory. "I thought they were rather well suited, but it petered out not long after starting."

Venus frowned. "This was while Oxander was away?"

Kim nodded. "Ursula and Oxander hadn't really hit it off at that time yet."

Nodding, Venus reread his notes. Laughing with his

thoughts, he saw Kim look at him questionably. "This reads rather like a soap opera script." He explained.

Kim too laughed. "I like Nolan, for what it's worth." He added. "After we lost Roger, I asked Nolan if he needed any help with the workload, but he refused. He said it wasn't necessary and he could cope. Not many people would do that."

Venus nodded again. Was it admirable, or did it mean that Nolan had something to hide? As much as he shared Kim's idea that the young fisherman was likeable, there were a lot of loose ends...

David shook his head sorrowfully. He would have much preferred a party than another wake at the Inn. His solemn mood was felt around the island, the mourners taking a drink in Ursula's memory were quiet and thoughtful.

He would never have thought that Quentin would have fallen under Ursula's spell as many men had, and it had been proved that he hadn't. It seemed he had been captivated by her step-sister instead: Shona was the likeable, amenable sort - and he was struck with the thought that the couple could be very well suited. If only they would let each other in...

"Thank you," Shona hesitated at the door to the tiny flat above the shop she called home. "You didn't have to walk me home."

Quentin gave her a smile. "It's no problem. I wanted to make sure that you were alright after everything that happened."

Smiling at him, she winced as her split lip protested. The trickle of fresh blood caused her to curse.

In a flash, Quentin had a cotton handkerchief held up to her mouth. "Hold that there for a few minutes, it'll soon calm."

Was he always so practical and caring, Shona wondered. Her resolve to never let another man into her heart was weakening the more time they spent together, which was ludicrous as they must have only been in each other's company for around a few hours at the most. It did feel like it was far longer, and not in a bad way...

"Get some rest." He advised her. "I'm going to be around tomorrow so I'll check on you sometime." He hesitated. "Of course, if that is okay with you?"

Was that his way of asking her out? Shona wondered. Realising that he was waiting for an answer, she nodded and thanked him.

Chapter 43

"They broke in, but didn't take anything?" Venus asked Walter when he came to the office with the news that overnight the shop on Harbourtown had been broken into.

"That's right. Damn strange." Walter mused, scratching his head.

"That means they either found what they wanted, they knew where to look, or they didn't know and didn't find whatever it was they were after." Hesitating, Venus pondered an idea. "Was it to just give us a red herring?"

"A red herring?" Walter laughed.

"It's not such a silly idea. The murderer is becoming nervous because he knows we are onto him."

Walter gaped. "We are?"

Venus nodded. "We are."

Still staring at him, Walter frowned. "You said 'he', how do you know we're after a man?"

"I have a feeling, that's all, nothing concrete." Venus frowned.

The fact that everyone seemed to have a perfect alibi had to be smashed somewhere. There was a flaw, it just had to be found.

Isaac looked kindly at Shona when they met the next morning in the shop. "How did you sleep? You look very tired. Perhaps you should have the day off." He suggested.

Wearily, Shona sighed. Had he been sent to see how she was? If so, she thought that his parents were probably behind it. "My head is thumping," she confessed.

He nodded. "Aside from the stress of it all, are you okay after the fall?"

Choosing his words carefully, he knew he was on rocky ground asking after her welfare. Hearing about Shona's collapse at the service, he felt even more sorry for her - and this morning he could see the bruises were coming out on her pale face. He didn't want her to think that he was trying to pry.

"Mum was very worried about you, Dad too." He added.

She treated him to her brave smile. "They are wonderful, your Mum and Dad."

"And Quentin," Isaac pointed out, "we saw he took you home last night. I'm glad they were all looking after you."

Shona flinched.

Immediately he apologised. "We weren't spying."

"I know." She gave him a small smile, careful not to disturb the cut on her lip again as she had done last night several times. "You can't have helped seeing us when Quentin very kindly walked me home." She sighed then. "I'm very grateful to you all, honestly."

"Good." He gave her one of his trademark grins, holding out his hand. "Then I insist. Have the day off, leave me the keys and I'll see to anyone who wants anything."

"Isaac no!" Shona gasped. "You are far too busy."

He shrugged. "We can cope. Cecil is a natural." He saw she was being swayed by the idea. "Go on. It'll be okay. You can check up on me later if you want." He teased.

"I know I don't need to do that." Shona took the shop keys from her pocket, weighing them in her hand thoughtfully. "If you are absolutely sure," she paused.

"I am." He nodded, stepping towards her and taking them from her hand before she could change her mind. "Go on."

Hugging him and thanking him, she walked out by his side, watching him lock up. Stepping into the side entrance to the flat above the shop and closing the door over behind her, she let go of a huge sigh.

"I haven't seen her," Isaac frowned. "Not since this morning when I sent her back to the apartment to rest." He looked at Quentin fearfully. "Do you suppose she's okay? I meant to check up on her but it's been so busy." He nodded at the wall between the pub and the shop. "I took the keys off her before I sent her to rest."

Quentin smiled at him. "That was very kind of you. I'm sure she was grateful."

"Oh, she was." Isaac nodded. "I feel for her, all this, it's such a horrid business." He sighed. "Are you busy, at the moment, I mean, you're always busy. Could you check on her, for me, please? Set my mind at rest."

"I have time." Quentin smiled. "Will she be asleep, do you think? She might not hear me knocking."

Isaac smiled at him and handed over a bundle of keys. "That larger one is the flat key. Untangle it in case I need to get into the shop while you're gone." He disappeared when his name was called. "Leave the bunch behind the bar." He added, over his shoulder.

"Will do." Quentin nodded, deftly locating the right key and untwisting it from the keyring. "I'll let you know how she is." He added, but Isaac had already gone.

Earlier he had wondered how he was going to get to see Shona when he'd seen that the shop was closed. The handwritten note on the door pointed him to The Empty Tankard next door for any enquiries, and he'd known then that a plan had been made.

Initially, he was there on business - after her collapse in the church during the service yesterday, he wanted to check up on her. He also wanted to know personally how she was doing - grief did strange things to the mind if left to take over.

A part of him was worried about her; his heart told him to go to her. Of course he had no idea what he was going to say when he was in the apartment with her, but he'd cross that bridge when he came to it.

Tired and tousled, Shona answered the door after the short ringing on the bell. She had half wondered if it would be Tanya, or maybe Isaac, wanting to see how she was. Completely thrown by Quentin's presence on her doorstep, she wrapped her dressing gown around her a bit more tightly, suddenly feeling very under dressed.

"Come in," she spoke immediately, ushering him inside and shutting the door behind them.

For an awkward moment, they stood looking at each other, each trying to find their tongue.

"Go through." Shona shooed him jokingly. "I should have expected a house call." She teased, glad when he laughed. "Although, if I'd known you were coming..." Gesturing vaguely at her attire, her words ran out.

"I'm sorry, I should have said that I intended to visit." He similarly trailed off. He was glad then that he'd rung the bell and waited, instead of using the key.

Looking into each other's eyes, he smiled kindly at her.

She returned the smile. "Are you here to check up on me by any chance?"

"Guilty as charged." He laughed, holding up his hands in mock defence. "How do you feel?"

"Tired, sore," she yawned carefully as if to prove the point, "and embarrassed." Her smile disappeared. "You are far too busy to be stopping to check up on me."

"Not everyone gets special treatment." He joked. "Otherwise, you're right, I'd have no time at all."

"Sit down," she waved him into the chair, "unless you can't stop? I was going to make tea." Shona hesitated.

"I have a suitable gap in my schedule for tea." He joked once more.

She nodded and disappeared into the next room, which he followed her into, finding it was a small kitchen with a table to one side. Sitting at the table so that they could continue to talk, he watched as she collected up the necessary.

"Sugar?" She offered.

"No, thanks." He pulled a face. "My first wife told me that I was sweet enough." Seeing the shock across her face, he apologised. "I'm sorry you didn't ask to know that." He laughed at himself, trying to drown out his own embarrassment.

"Nonetheless, I'll remember." She replied, stirring the mug before placing it in front of him. Then she realised what she'd said! "I mean, that you don't take sugar. For next time." She winced, and flinched. "Assuming there is a next time." She added.

"Yes." He didn't know what to say, other than to agree.

"It's very..."

"I wanted..."

They both began to talk at the same time. Both stopped and apologised, and asked the other to start. Then they both laughed, and Shona flinched again as her bruised face protested.

"It'll take a few days before that calms down." He was looking at her intently.

"I was lucky really." She agreed then shuddered, sitting down opposite him at the table. "I apologise for the state of the place." She waved her hands around. "Yours must be a palace compared to this."

"It's nothing fancy." Quentin shrugged. "I need functionality not frivolity."

"That sounds like you." Shona nodded at him. "I mean, from what I know about you." She tried.

Quentin laughed. "We're not very good at this, are we? Who knew conversation was so damned hard." He joked, glad when she laughed.

Chapter 44

The two policemen were together once more in the office to discuss the case in private.

"I'm really not sure." Walter began. "I'm still no closer to finding any new information that could be of use." He gave a dejected sigh. "I don't believe Shona could do it. She didn't hate her that much, and she's a decent sort."

Thinking over the meeting with the lady in question, Venus had to agree. "Who does that leave us with, other than Quentin?"

"A lover?" Walter spoke the word cautiously.

"Or an ex-lover." Venus was aware that both Nolan and Oxander had been at the top of his list from early on.

Walter nodded at the idea. Suddenly, the thought hit him: Walter gasped. "No, that can't be right. Nolan is innocent, I'm sure, as is Quentin. You don't honestly think it was either of them?"

Venus shrugged. "I have faith in the good Doctor, certainly."

"Quentin definitely wouldn't have done it. I saw his face when he arrived at the scene - he was shocked, that wasn't an act." Walter insisted.

Nodding and steepling his fingers in front of him, Venus watched the thought processes glide across Walter's features.

"That only leaves Oxander. But it can't be him, he loved her." Walter stated. "Besides, he was in the lighthouse during the storm." His brow furrowed.

Venus cleared his throat noisily. "So he maintains, but there is no actual proof of that. Even if he was, there was plenty of opportunity for him to slip out of the lighthouse, do the deed and return without anyone seeing him."

Walter gasped again. "That makes far better sense than

Nolan." He nodded after a few moments of silent contemplation.

"It wouldn't be the first crime of passion, whichever one of them it was." Venus pointed out, waiting until Walter nodded before continuing. "Now we have to wait for him to make a mistake that will reveal himself to us."

"Huh?" Walter was beyond confused. "What sort of mistake?"

Venus smiled at him. "Of that, I am not yet sure." He grimaced. "What if there is a connection to the deaths of Roger and Ursula?"

Stopping himself in time, Walter managed not to roll his eyes. Almost since they had met, Inspector Venus had been determined that the two deaths were somehow connected - he was like a dog with a bone, he wouldn't give it up!

"Nolan was not responsible for Roger's death." He began, slowly. "Even if he wanted to extract revenge, he wouldn't have done anything so dangerous."

Venus's eyebrows raised. "Why would he want to extract revenge?"

And so, Walter told him what he himself had only recently discovered. This necessitated another interview with the young fisherman.

"Nolan, Nolan," Venus clicked his tongue loudly, shaking his head. "Did you not think I would find out?"

Nolan's expression was frightened. "Find out what?"

Eyeing him, Venus allowed the tension to settle in the room. "Your partnership with Roger wasn't equal, was it? He promised you equal shares of the best of the catch; the best of the customers. But you didn't get it."

He got up to walk around the table, standing beside the chair Nolan was perched on. Continuing to question him, he watched the young man's face carefully. "When did you discover Roger had been swindling you?"

Nolan remained quiet.

"How long did you keep it to yourself that he was mistreating you; disrespecting you?" Venus pressed.

"A while," he spoke shakily, "Mr Venus, I didn't..."

"You didn't what?" Venus leant towards him. "You didn't mean to kill him?"

Nolan shook his head. "I didn't kill him." He insisted strongly. "I would never have done Roger any harm. I was annoyed at first, but I could understand what he did." Nolan took a deep breath. "I'd have done the same if the roles were reversed." He confessed. "This was his territory, not mine. His family have fished these waters exclusively for generations. He was bound to be upset by having to share what he had been told forever was his." At that point, he looked Venus in the eyes. "Wouldn't you have felt the same?"

Venus had to admit that he was impressed with the young man; and relieved that Nolan wasn't the bad sort. He had seen it many times before, and it was never pleasant.

"Is that why when you were asked if you wanted any help, you refused?" Venus remembered something then he'd learned from the conversation with Kim.

"Maybe." Nolan shrugged. "I like keeping busy. It's long, hard work. It's not for everyone, but I like it."

After a pause, Venus recalled something Nolan had said the last time they'd met. "You would continue to live this life even if you had the choice to leave?"

"I haven't decided yet." He shrugged, his gaze falling to the floor. "I've been trying to not think about it."

"You will need to decide at some point, Nolan."

He sighed. It was a deep, heartfelt sigh. "I know." When he looked up again, Venus saw with shock that Nolan looked older than his years. "I'm glad you understand about Roger. I knew if people found out that I'd be blamed for his death. I truly don't know why he was out in that weather. I hope to God he didn't suffer much."

Walking to the door, Venus held it open for him. "I hope so too." He replied, patting him on the shoulder.

Chapter 45

Tanya heard the Inspector's voice on the other side of the door. It sounded like he was talking to someone, despite the fact that she was sure he was alone. Walter had left earlier, and no interviews were currently being undertaken, she was sure.

Knocking first, she waited to be invited in before she entered. "I'm sorry to interrupt," she began, her eye falling on Vimto sitting in the opposite chair. "Oh, is he in your way?"

"No need to worry, he's fine." Venus told her. "He is a very good listener. I'm reviewing the notes I've made for the case so far." He nodded at his feline companion. "He's helping." Venus gave her a smile.

She laughed aloud. "Vimto, Assistant Detective." She tried it. "Sounds great." Ruffling the fur on his neck, she told him to behave himself.

"He is very well behaved for a stray."

Tanya shrugged. "He came across from the mainland one day with Yves and decided he liked it better here. He's no longer a stray, we all look after him."

"Especially now you've moved out of the lighthouse." Venus told the cat. "You're spoiled here, I'd say."

Vimto purred loudly as if to concur.

Satisfied, Tanya left them to it. Talking to Vimto was something everyone did. She dismissed her doubts about the Inspector's sanity.

"So, Vimto." Venus addressed the cat. "A quick recap."

The cat turned his head away, as if to shirk him. Venus laughed.

"Our main suspects are Shona, Walter, Quentin, Kim, Nolan and Oxander. I'm not convinced that Nolan would have it in him, so I'm taking him off the list."

"Meow." He agreed.

"Likewise, I doubt any of the Treduggan family were involved."

"Meow."

"Including Kim." Waiting for the corresponding meow, Venus continued when it came. "Walter too, although he could have done it, I don't see why he would."

"Meow."

"That leaves us with the step-sister, the lover and the doctor. Usually it is a family member or a lover, old or new, and I'm inclined to believe my instinct that Quentin isn't the murderer."

"Meow!" Vimto agreed loudly.

"That leaves us with Shona and Oxander. Both have motives, and both were alone at the time of death."

Losing interest, Vimto began to sniff the air.

"What's up? What can you smell?" Venus too lost his chain of thought.

David's office was alongside the Inn's kitchen; consulting his watch, Venus realised that they were starting to cook for the lunchtime menu.

The medium ferocity of the early evening storm presented a perfect opportunity for the Harbourtown RNLI team of Oxander, Yves, Nolan and Quentin to complete a training exercise.

Venus silently wished them a safe and successful journey, watching from the office window overlooking the harbour. He was not alone, as Vimto was also there.

"You know, Vimto." Venus began, the thought striking him. "With the harbourmaster out, we could explore your lighthouse without interruption."

"Meow!" He exclaimed, jumping down from the window seat.

"I'm sure it would help." Venus mused. "There's something I can't put my finger on about Felix and his keeper."

The sound of scratching at the door made Venus look - the cat was clawing at the door, as if he wanted out.

"You can't possibly go out in this weather." Going over to him, Venus stroked Vimto's head as it was thrust into his outstretched hand. "Besides, your poor paw would get soaked."

The idea struck Venus then.

"You stay here, I'll go."

"Meow!" Vimto agreed.

Asking to borrow some waterproof clothing, Tanya was amazed the Inspector intended to go out in such foul weather. Nonetheless, she obliged; within ten minutes, Venus was making strides towards the lighthouse in slightly oversized wet weather gear belonging to David.

Although he was by no means unfit, Venus was out of breath from battling the wind and the rain by the time he reached the foot of the monstrous iron tower. Glancing towards the harbour opening, there was no sign of the lifeboat returning, so he pursued the chance.

Heaving for breath at the top of the twisty steps, his remaining breath was stolen by the dramatic view. Oxander had been right when he'd described the scene - there was sight of almost everywhere from up there. Eye falling on the Treduggan house on the hill, Venus could also imagine the views that Kim saw through his telescope. But he wasn't here to admire the view.

He needed to find what he was looking for, although he didn't know quite what that was. The machinery around the observation deck was too clean, he noticed, almost as if it were new.

Lights flashed; buzzers sounded; the foghorn triggered as the clouds came rolling in. Deafened by it, Venus wondered how Oxander still had his hearing.

Then a message lit up the central console: **Automated System Receiving.**

The smile curled around Venus's lips. The harbourmaster's ironclad alibi was ruined with this discovery - Venus patted the side of the lighthouse in a congratulatory way. They had their murderer!

Having watched from the window, Vimto knew where the Inspector had been and knew when he was returning to the Inn.

Shedding sodden layers before properly going inside, so as not to soak the floors and anyone he came across, Venus was grinning from ear to ear.

"You are such a clever boy!" Venus exclaimed, dropping to his knees to cuddle the hunk of fur and purring of Vimto when he was greeted at the door by the cat.

Tanya came in as Venus scooped Vimto into his arms. "Err..." She hesitated. "Did you find what you wanted?" She enquired politely.

"I sure did." Grinning jubilantly at her, she must have thought Venus had lost his mind, he acknowledged how strange his behaviour seemed. "Can I check something with you?"

Carefully placing Vimto down on the sofa before turning to her, Venus spoke cautiously, almost as if he was worried about what her reply would tell him.

"There was work done at the lighthouse recently, wasn't there?"

From her expression, Tanya was confused what this had relevance to, or indeed what it meant. "Some six weeks or so ago. Why? Is that important?"

Venus nodded and thanked her, dashing out of the room to bound up the stairs to the Inn's guest accommodation area, and banging on Walter's door.

Walter was not pleased at the interruption, but listened patiently, his eyes widening as time went on.

"We've got him!" He exclaimed triumphantly. "That bastard!" He growled.

"Now, Walter." Venus warned, able to read his mind. "Let the magistrate deal with him. No justice is done with our fists."

"Of course." Walter muttered, unconvincingly Venus had to admit. "Shall I bring him in when they get back?"

Venus contemplated the idea for a moment. "Let's wait until morning. We might need back up if he were to turn violent."

Walter nodded his agreement, although Venus could see he was far from placated.

Chapter 46

The next morning, Walter fetched Oxander to the office early. They walked along the quay side by side in silence - Walter managed to contain himself, the Inspector's words of warning rolling around in his head.

When they arrived, Walter didn't retreat from the office as before.

Undeterred by this, Oxander let the note flitter down onto the table in front of the two policemen. "I found this, and I thought you both should see it."

Walter edged closer, peering at the slip of paper. He snorted. Venus looked at him and he mumbled an apology.

"You found it, you say? Where?" Venus asked, barely reading the note.

Oxander seemed thrown by this question. "Does it matter?"

"If the Inspector asks you, then yes, it does matter." Walter chided him. "Answer the question."

"Erm... Blowing along the quay. Must've been in someone's pocket, or in a boat."

"Someone?" Venus checked, looking again at the note. "It is for Nolan, so assuming that he received it, then it is his."

"Of course he received it. How else would it have been around?" Oxander's expression was scornful.

"It could have been planted." Venus replied matter of factly. "It doesn't sound very genuine to me." He skimmed over the words on the supposed love note.

'Nolan, don't be jealous, I don't love you and you can't make me change my mind. You should move on. I love another. Ursula.'

Steam virtually poured from Oxander's ears. "How can you

say that? How do you know?"

"How do you know?" Venus spun the question back at him.

"I... I..." He stuttered. "They had an affair while I wasn't here. That's proof."

Shaking his head, Venus saw Walter was also doing the same.

"They had a brief affair, there was no love." Walter corrected.

Oxander gaped like a fish out of water. "But this proves that Nolan was jealous..."

"No. It doesn't." Venus stated. "For all we know this could be fake."

"Fake?" Oxander's eyes widened.

Something in the back of Venus's mind clicked. The shop had been broken into not long after he had arrived but nothing had been taken. However! If someone had wanted to forge the victim's handwriting, they would have needed an example to copy from. It all made sense now!

"Not long ago, the shop was broken into but nothing visibly had been taken." Venus informed him, watching Oxander's reaction. "Therefore, I'd say it was a safe assumption that the burglar and the author of the note are the same." He turned to Walter. "Would you agree?"

"I would." Walter nodded. "We were puzzled over why it had taken place, now it's obvious."

Oxander went as white as a sheet.

"So!" Getting to his feet, Venus walked around the table to stand beside him. "I reckon your fanciful theory is, in fact, a lie."

"You can't know. You haven't found the murder weapon yet." Oxander tried, his voice weak.

"Haven't we?" Venus briefly glanced at Walter and winked. "Who gave you that information?"

Oxander's face fell even more.

"Whoever it was, they were misinformed. In fact, I am pleased to say that we have sufficient information to warrant an arrest."

Audibly, Oxander gasped. And then tried to hide it. "Wow, I mean, that's amazing. You found out who's alibi didn't wash."

"It didn't take long once we established the facts." Venus strung out the sentence.

"Nothing takes long once you have all the facts." Walter added.

Oxander was now looking between them, his expression that of a caged animal.

"Oxander Knowe," Venus began.

Attempting to run for it, Venus tripped him before Oxander reached the door. Walter pounced on the culprit with a stealth Venus hadn't seen before, pulling Oxander's arms tightly behind his back while he was treated to the usual arresting statement and handcuffed. Perhaps he was rougher than necessary, but Venus didn't interfere: his comrade's expression was calm, so he knew there would be no brutality on his part.

Silently thankful, he gave the signal to the waiting men outside. "Walter, if you would." Venus gestured to the door. "The mainland police truck is waiting for us."

Together, they marched the culprit outside, handing him over to the Police Commissioner - the same man who had lectured Walter months previously. The Commissioner congratulated them as the truck left for the harbour; Yves had the hovercraft waiting to transfer them to the mainland.

Watching their departure, Venus felt a deep satisfaction.

Chapter 47

"How could he?!" Shona virtually howled. "That bastard!!" Fists clenched tightly, tears of rage pouring down her cheeks, she half sobbed, half screamed.

Quentin had taken over from Walter, given the circumstances and how they both thought Shona might react. He hadn't expected her to be doing this: he wasn't very sure what to say next. After all, he was used to giving bad news in his job, sometimes.

After several minutes of helplessly watching, he went over to her and put his arms around her. "I know." He said softly in her ear.

The anger drained from her, leaving her now sobbing against his shoulder. Taking a few steps sideways with her, he sat them both down on the sofa.

A very long time later, she began to calm: still he kept his arms around her. "Quentin, I..."

"Sshh," he shushed her. "No need to say anything."

"But..."

He gave her a kind smile. "No buts." Giving her a gentle squeeze, he then let her go. "I took over from Walter, I didn't want anyone else to tell you."

"Thank you." She sniffed. "That's very good of you." Looking up, she saw he was looking into her face. His kindness - his words, his look, his gestures - set her off crying again.

Bundling her against him, he cursed as his phone began to ring. Hastily digging about in his pocket with one hand for it, he located the off button. The call would have to wait.

Walter grasped Venus's hand tightly. "I want to thank you for everything."

Venus could see from his face that he wanted to say a lot more, so he kept quiet.

"You showed me that I need to persevere in the face of the impossible. I'd never encountered anything like this before, and I couldn't get past the idea that Ursula was gone." His face fell.

"Police work is harder when there's a personal angle." Venus reminded him. "I am grateful to you for making yourself available to me. Together we succeeded."

Walter nodded.

"I hope that you never encounter something like this again." Venus added. "It is certainly not a part of the job that I will miss."

Walter's expression changed. "You're leaving the force?"

"Early retirement." Venus laughed. "I've earned it."

Walter nodded his agreement. "You will have had a successful career over the years, no doubt."

Deciding it was best to skim over the details, Venus nodded and smiled.

"Anyway," Walter was shaking his hand again. "Thank you for straightening me out."

"You're too good a man to waste." Venus spoke truthfully.

Walter seemed to grow three inches at that.

"It will do you well to remember that. Keep up the good work, Walter." Untangling his hand, Venus nodded readiness to Yves, who had held up the scheduled leaving time so Walter could say goodbye.

He waved passionately after them, and Venus gave him a small wave in return.

"You'll be relieved to be going home." Yves said after a few moments of silence - if it was at all possible to have silence on board a hovercraft.

"I am." Venus grinned at him. "Retirement awaits." Rubbing

his hands together gleefully, the thought struck that he was yet to give a report to the Superintendent before packing up his desk for the last time. But that was a minor point...

"We have a replacement harbourmaster already." Yves spoke as the mainland came into view.

"Pierre?" Venus guessed, laughing at Yves's shocked expression. "Not much of a mystery that - he enjoyed his brief time here, and who wouldn't? Some would say Harbourtown is idyllic, if you like that sort of thing."

Yves laughed. "I couldn't live in the city now." He screwed his face up with disgust. "All the grime and dirt. No, give me the sea air any time."

"And the love of a good woman." Venus reminded him. "You have the best business partner."

"I do." He smiled thinking about Caitlin. "Are you in a... I mean, I don't mean to pry."

"It's okay, I'm not offended." Venus replied, his gaze drifting to the horizon as he spoke. "There was once."

"It's never too late to love again." Yves stated. "As Shona and Quentin are discovering."

Venus genuinely smiled. "A great man you have there in Quentin. You'd do well to keep him on side."

"We are very fortunate that he chose this area to move to." Yves agreed. "But we can't keep him here."

"If what you say is true, Shona can." Venus pointed out.

They lapsed into silence as he docked, or parked, or whatever you do with a hovercraft. Beached, perhaps? Shaking Venus's hand, Yves thanked him for solving the murder and wished him well in retirement. Likewise, Venus wished him well for the future.

The Superintendent had called them misfits, nitwits and eejits - but as far as Venus could tell, the only one that fit the description was the culprit.

Stopping off at the police station on the mainland, Venus was in time to listen in to the interview with Oxander. If he knew what was good for him, he would confess the whole thing without delay.

But who knew what he was thinking? Venus certainly hadn't pegged him as the murderous type, but even the most mild mannered person can snap in a rage. This, Venus suspected, was what had happened.

Handcuffed to the side of the interview table, Oxander had a sunken demeanour. Answering the basic questions about his identity and his need to understand what his rights were, he didn't otherwise speak.

Once prompted, he began to talk about what had occurred that night. His voice was clear but soft, as if he was in a sort of trance.

"As the storm rolled in, the rain began. The heavens opened. I tried to send her home, but she wouldn't go. She wouldn't leave me. She kept a tight hold on me. She was saying things that I didn't want to hear, but I couldn't block it out. Her words were louder as the storm became louder: she was shouting at me, and I was shouting at her. I don't know what happened next..." He trailed off. Swallowing hard, he took a deep breath. "I told her to leave me alone. She said no. She turned her back to me, blocking the path so I couldn't go. We've had so many storms recently the boats were close to the harbour edge as the water level was so high. The lightning picked out the boat hook on the nearest boat, and I grabbed it.

I only wanted to frighten her, I didn't actually intend to use it. But she didn't want to listen to me, she didn't move, she said neither of us were going anywhere until I listened to what she had to say. I reacted. It was... automatic, like an

219

instinct, a reflex." He shrugged. "I watched, like slow motion watching, as the hook smashed into her head, and her body went limp." Tears in freefall down his face, he lost his voice.

Behind the one-way glass in the next room, Venus nodded to himself.

"What happened after that?" The policeman holding the interview prompted.

"I..." He sniffed, closed his eyes and swallowed several times. "I panicked. I didn't mean to do anything. First, I checked, but she was dead. There was no pulse. I couldn't get help, there was no point, she was beyond help." He took several shuddery breaths. "I had no idea what to do next. The storm was worsening with each minute, and nobody was around. I ran to the lighthouse as I usually would. Numbly, I hung up my waterproofs on the hook behind the door as usual and went up the steps to the top. I was in a daze. I didn't know what to do."

The interviewer consulted his notes. "After that, you raised the alarm. You were there when Dr Farma ruled her as dead. He thought that she may have hit her head on the cobbles as they can be treacherously slippery in wet weather." He looked up at Oxander. "That was when you seized the opportunity of covering up your crime. Why did you not confess the truth then?"

"I panicked. I was still in a panic, and in shock at what had happened."

The interviewer was not at all happy with this response, Venus could see. "At what stage did you get rid of the evidence? The boat hook you used would have been stained with blood."

"I kicked it off the quayside into the water." Oxander admitted, his head hung in shame.

The interviewer frowned. "Did the owner of the boat not

realise that it was missing?"

Oxander shook his head. "They float. It wouldn't have gone far. The rain would have washed it, and the quayside, clean."

"How convenient!" The interviewer sat back in the chair. "And you knew this?"

Oxander shrugged. "I didn't think about it." He admitted. "I could hardly think straight."

There was a pause.

"But yes." He said.

The second police officer in the room exchanged words with the interviewer quietly.

Venus had seen enough. There was no need to stay any longer - and there was a lengthy interview ahead of him with the Superintendent. Signing over to the local police, Venus was relieved to make his way into the fresh air. The matter was now out of his hands, and life at Harbourtown could resume its picturesque peacefulness.

Chapter 48

With the murder solved, and Pierre as Oxander's permanent replacement, it didn't take much to get regular activities at Harbourtown resumed.

Yves had the pleasure of working on the contract to have a lifeboat shop at Bountiful Bay, on the hard standing by the beach. This was the better idea of all that were put forward for the space, the community agreed, nominating Shona to manage the venture.

He ensured that photographs and artwork of the surrounding areas, as well as general provisions, were on sale to the general public - aware that this worked well for all involved. Most pleased that Shona had been appointed to run it, he knew the new business was in experienced hands.

Likewise the shop by The Empty Tankard was in good hands - a cut through had been made between the two premises, and a member of the bar staff was present to take orders from the shop's customers.

Shona had a new location for her business but also a new home with a fabulous view. The beach view at Bountiful Bay was beautiful at both sunrise and sunset; she counted her blessings that her peaceful life had resumed.

A special visit from the Scilly Islands celebrity, Mr Justin Thyme, took place next. He had put off his visit in the murder aftermath and was dissuaded from visiting while filming by the Cornish Tourist Centre took place.

Little did they know that he also wanted to film, and he had the idea to develop a bird observatory in the not so distant future at Harbourtown. He explained that a bird observatory was a centre for the study of bird migration and bird populations, usually focusing on local birds, but may also include interest in far-flung areas.

Caitlin, Yves and Kim were beyond thrilled; instantly agreeing.

Once his paw had healed, Vimto split his time between the lighthouse and the Inn, taking extra feeding wherever he could as he always had. He took well to Pierre, and likewise Pierre to him - they were seen together on several different occasions on the observation deck of the lighthouse and once more, the catly shadow could be seen at times when the beacon was flashing.

Mostly, Vimto spent the nights at the Inn with Tanya and David - so much so, David had a cat flap installed in the back door. He said it was to keep his wife happy, but even Tanya knew David had developed a soft spot for the feline.

Thanks to his detective work, he'd earned himself a reputation amongst the guests and visitors as well as the villagers. As such, he played a starring role in the film that was made in Harbourtown. The legend of the Mousehole cat brought tourists there, and Vimto became the Harbourtown equivalent - only he was still alive to enjoy the fuss and extra treats!

Books by Yvonne Marrs

Introduction to the Fictional Work of Yvonne Marrs

When The Sax Man Plays Part 1 - Making It

When The Sax Man Plays Part 2 - Proving It

When The Sax Man Plays Part 3 - Managing It

When The Sax Man Plays Part 4 - His Return

When The Sax Man Plays Part 5 - The Prequel

When The Sax Man Plays ...and All That Jazz

Football Crazy 1: A World Cup Adventure

Football Crazy 2: On The Edge of Glory

Football Crazy 3: The Hat-trick

Football Crazy 4: A Point to Prove

Football Crazy 5: The Master of Managerial Psychology

Aiden Lewis Octet Book 1 - Memoirs

Aiden Lewis Octet Book 2 - Reminiscence

Aiden Lewis Octet Book 3 - Touring

Aiden Lewis Octet Book 4 - Bravado

Aiden Lewis Octet Book 5 - Partnership

Aiden Lewis Octet Book 6 - Vulnerable

Aiden Lewis Octet Book 7 - Struggles

Aiden Lewis Octet Book 8 - Denouement

Undeserved 1

Undeserved 2

Undeserved 3

Putting The Visible Into So-Called Invisible Illnesses
Through Poetry

Castiliano Vulgo - An Elizabethan Story

Harbourtown Murder

Inexorable

Termination at the Halt

Can't Buy Health 1

Can't Buy Health 2

Can't Buy Health 3

Can't Buy Health 4

Can't Buy Health 5

Can't Buy Health 6

Can't Buy Health 7

Can't Buy Health 8

We hope you have enjoyed this book,
please leave a review for Yvonne.

Printed in Great Britain
by Amazon

85434220R00129